A Message from Patrick to Deanna:

How to describe my feelings for you?

Eleven years of an endless honeymoon.
132 months of breakfast in bed.
3,984 days of wine and roses.
95,616 hours of making love by the sea.
5,736,960 minutes of enduring romance.
And 344,217,600 seconds of being with the one
who completes my soul.
Patrick + Deanna. Forever.

Patrick Combs wrote this to his wife,
Deanna Latson. His entry was chosen
from hundreds in the Harlequin Everlasting Love
contest held in March 2007. Participants were
asked to explain "What about your love makes it
everlasting?" The contest was a collaboration between
Harlequin and Sandals Resorts.

The couple—pictured on the cover of this book—
was flown to Mediterranean Village at Sandals
Grande Antigua Resort & Spa for the cover shoot.
That day in paradise will live in their memories, and
this piece of art commemorates their love, not just
on Valentine's Day but forever.

Patrick and Deanna, like authors Tara Taylor Quinn,
Jean Brashear and Linda Cardillo, know that every
great love has a story to tell!

ABOUT THE AUTHORS

With more than forty novels—published in twenty languages—to her credit, **Tara Taylor Quinn** is a *USA TODAY* bestselling author. She is known for her deeply emotional and psychologically astute stories. Tara is a three-time finalist for the Romance Writers of America's RITA® Award, a multiple finalist for the National Readers' Choice Award, the Reviewers' Choice Award, the Booksellers' Best Award and the Holt Medallion. Tara also writes romantic-suspense fiction for MIRA Books. Her next MIRA title, *At Close Range*, will appear in October 2008. When she's not writing or fulfilling speaking engagements, she enjoys traveling and spending time with her family (including several dogs!) and friends.

A letter to Rod Stewart resulting in a Cinderella birthday for her daughter sowed the seeds of **Jean Brashear**'s writing career. Since becoming published two years after she started her first book, she has appeared on the Waldenbooks bestseller list and been a finalist for or won numerous awards, including the RITA® Award, the *Romantic Times BOOKreviews* Reviewers Choice, National Readers Choice and others. A lifelong avid reader, she still finds it thrilling each time she sees her name on the cover of a new book.

Before she became a novelist, **Linda Cardillo** wrote several works of nonfiction, from articles in the *New York Times* to business texts on marketing and corporate policy. Between earning her Harvard MBA and publishing her first novel, she's had careers in publishing, teaching and development. She still owns the dictionary she won as first prize in a library essay contest when she was twelve years old. She has many more stories to tell and is currently finishing her next work of fiction. Her first novel was the acclaimed *Dancing on Sunday Afternoons*, published by Harlequin Everlasting Love.

THE VALENTINE GIFT

Tara Taylor Quinn

Jean Brashear

Linda Cardillo

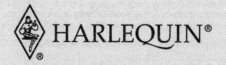

HARLEQUIN®

TORONTO • NEW YORK • LONDON
AMSTERDAM • PARIS • SYDNEY • HAMBURG
STOCKHOLM • ATHENS • TOKYO • MILAN • MADRID
PRAGUE • WARSAW • BUDAPEST • AUCKLAND

ISBN-13: 978-0-373-71465-0
ISBN-10: 0-373-71465-3

THE VALENTINE GIFT

Copyright © 2008 by Harlequin Books S.A.

The publisher acknowledges the copyright holders of the individual works as follows:

VALENTINE'S DAUGHTERS
Copyright © 2008 by Tara Taylor Quinn.

OUR DAY
Copyright © 2008 by Jean Brashear.

THE HAND THAT GIVES THE ROSE
Copyright © 2008 by Linda Cardillo Platzer.

This edition published by arrangement with Harlequin Books S.A.

® and TM are trademarks of the publisher. Trademarks indicated with ® are registered in the United States Patent and Trademark Office, the Canadian Trade Marks Office and in other countries.

www.eHarlequin.com

Printed in U.S.A.

CONTENTS

Dear Reader,

Happy Valentine's Day! I've always been fascinated by the bond that draws women in a family together—probably because I never had a sister and always wanted one! I have this idea that there's a current that runs between related females, originating in one place and linking them together in a way that cannot be broken. In my mind, this current is there to serve and protect a woman—to keep her heart safe in a world that is often painful. And the place it originates is home. Not home as in a building—walls and a kitchen table—but home in a larger sense. Something we can't touch, can't see, but can always somehow feel.

Not too long ago I was looking at life, at my life, and exploring this idea. "Valentine's Daughters" was the result of that introspection. Here is the story of three women, three generations of the same family, and how the current that runs through them holds them together, even when they've hardly met. I hope you enjoy the story as much as I enjoyed writing it.

I'd love to hear from you! Especially those of you who have sisters. Do you really feel the special bond I imagine?

You can reach me at www.tarataylorquinn.com or P.O. Box 13584, Mesa, AZ 85216.

Tara Taylor Quinn

VALENTINE'S DAUGHTERS

Tara Taylor Quinn

For the women in my family.
May we always be woven together.

CHAPTER ONE

February 13, 2008

"Ms. Slater, this is the New Hope Fertility Clinic calling to confirm your appointment for in vitro fertilization tomorrow afternoon at two...."

Shivering as she brushed snow off the sleeve of her cashmere coat, Monica Slater, newly separated from her husband, half listened as the young receptionist read a list of procedures over the answering machine before clicking off.

There were two other messages. They could wait.

Monica turned her attention from calls she didn't want to the mail she'd brought in from the box at the end of her drive, sure she didn't want it, either. Not even the bulky, eight-and-a-half-inch manila envelope.

The truth of the matter was, nothing sounded good at the moment. Not a hot-fudge sundae, a sinfully delicious steak or French fries. Not a chat with her best friend from college—or a vacation to Italy or the Caribbean. Not even a hot bath. Or a new car.

She was in a funk. Plain and simple.

The electric bill was paid. She'd done it online that morning. One envelope tossed. She didn't want a subscription to a new just-for-women magazine—even at the introductory price. Who cared if her favorite dress shop was having a fifty percent off sale to valued customers that weekend?

Or that she'd just closed the deal of her life that morning?

What did any of it matter? She was thirty years old. An investment broker at the top of her field—at least in Chicago's financial district—she owned a beautiful townhome in an elite gated community. Had more social invitations than she knew what to do with. Drove the car of her dreams—a Ford Expedition, Eddie Bauer luxury model—and was in perfect health.

And what did it all mean when the only voice that greeted her every night was a recording telling her how many messages she had?

At least the manila envelope distracted her for long enough to give her a five-second break from the relentless self-pity she'd been indulging in for most of the afternoon.

It was 4:00 p.m. on February 13th. Less than twelve hours until the first Valentine's Day she'd spent by herself since she'd met Shane ten years before.

Damn it.

A tear dripped onto the back of the envelope, turning the slightly gold color a deeper brown.

Flipping it over, Monica glanced at the return address.

Margaret Grace Warren. Her sixty-year-old paternal aunt. The woman who'd alternately blessed Monica's life—and driven her crazy. Monica had been sixteen when Aunt Margaret moved in with them, taking over the household duties, and leaning on Monica's dad— her older brother—more and more for emotional and financial support. But, until five years ago, she'd been the only mother figure Monica had ever known. She was still living in their family house in Tennessee—five years after Monica's unmarried father, Chris Warren, had passed away.

Almost thirty years after the death of Carol Bailey— Monica's mother.

Monica had talked to Aunt Margaret the previous week.

CURIOSITY DISPELLING self-pity for a second, Monica slid open the envelope. A small, light-brown leather book, wrapped and tied with a thin leather strap, fell out—smelling of age and…something else.

Running her fingers over the softness of its cover, Monica slowly untied the book's strap, careful when it started to fray. Obviously this was something of her father's. But what?

And why hadn't Aunt Margaret called before sending it?

The pages in the small bound book cracked as they pulled away from their binding. The ink was faded.

And the writing definitely wasn't her father's. It was smaller, rounder. A woman's handwriting. Or a child's.

With a gentle flip through the pages, Monica noticed the dates first. One at the top of each page. Starting with the year before she was born.

Then she saw the words *my baby* and sank to the floor.

CHAPTER TWO

January 25, 1977

Dear Diary,

I talked to Chris again last night. Mom and Dad were out playing bingo at the Senior Center. I know I shouldn't keep calling him. Or, at least, my head knows I shouldn't. But my heart just doesn't agree and I can't fight that. Truth be told, I don't want to fight my love for Chris. It feels so right that nothing else matters.

Everyone thinks I'm too young. But I turned eighteen two months ago. I'm a legal adult. And for a few months, until his birthday, I'm only nine years younger than Chris instead of ten.

Oh, Dearest Diary, am I being stupid? Listening to my heart when it's telling me that this is the love of my life? THE ONE?

Chris says we have to wait until I'm a little older, until I graduate from high school, go to college, but when I ask, he can't deny that he cares for me. He won't say he does. But he can't say he doesn't. He just gets this look in his eyes—those brown eyes that hide so much—and then he smiles at me and tells me to grow up fast.

We didn't talk all that long last night. His mother was awake and in pain and besides he keeps telling me that we have to be careful, that it's not right to have this friendship without Mom and Dad knowing. I keep telling him that all my life I've watched out for them as much as they have me, but I don't think he really believes me. How could he? His mom is younger than they are.

He'll be coming into the drugstore tomorrow to pick up the next batch of injections for his mom. I don't know how he does it, Dearest Diary. Staying in that tiny little apartment by the hospital. Watching her fade away like that.

It'll be better for him when his sister finishes school in Europe and comes home to help him. She'll be here in March and I know Chris is hoping his mother lasts that long.

I hope so, too.

But I also worry about what's going to happen when Margaret's here in Chicago. Will Chris really go back to the family home in Tennessee like he said? Take back the teaching job he's on sabbatical from?

I'll just die if he does. Or I'll follow him. There's no other choice.

I can't live without him.

February 13, 2008, 4:22 p.m.

WITH HER GAZE still on the page, on her mother's scrawled handwriting, absorbing far more than what was written there, Monica made her way into the living room, climbing into Shane's soft suede recliner, as she tried to connect the words she'd just read with the people she knew and loved.

Odd to see her beloved grandparents described as old back in 1977. Made them seem much older than their eighty-eight and ninety-two years, respectively. Aunt Margaret at school in Europe? Her aunt hadn't left their small Tennessee town in the past twenty years.

And Chris?

Given Monica's perception of her father as she remembered him—an aging schoolteacher who never got too excited about anything—she found it nearly impossible to fathom this account of a young man who'd inspired such passion. About as impossible as putting the leather notebook down.

January 26, 1977

It's me again. I feel like a completely different person than I did last night. Today was the best—and the worst. I wore my new denim miniskirt—the one I had to fight with Mom to be allowed to buy—and my striped blue-and-brown-and-white sweater with my brown boots. It wasn't really cold out today, thank goodness. I saw Chris's eyes darken when he first saw me. Like he wanted me. Like this hunger I feel for him is inside him, too.

The feeling was so powerful, Diary. So *real*. He wasn't looking at me like I was too young. But rather, like I was the only woman in the world for him. My whole body flooded with love and I forgot where we were. Even forgot for a second that we're staying "just friends" for now.

Then he looked away and I wanted to die. To run to him. To make him acknowledge this craziness between us. I *know* he felt it, too. He's taking this damned chivalry thing too far. I'm so scared that he's going to blow the chance of a lifetime for us. The one great love.

And all because of a few birthdays?

Doesn't he get that I'm not like everyone else? That I'm not a kid? Growing up the only child of people old enough to be your grandparents is great in some ways. You get all the attention and love and support you could ever want. But you learn to love books more than rock music, to watch the news instead of *Sesame Street*. And to be prepared to hear doctor's reports at the dinner table, holding your breath, hoping their bodies aren't deteriorating yet. That your folks will make it and live another thirty or forty years.

You grow up fast. And you learn very quickly to discern what matters most.

Love, Dearest Diary. That's what matters most. And finding someone to share it with for a lifetime and beyond. A love like Mom and Dad's.

Mom was only eleven when they met. And eighteen when they married. My age now.

I've never told Chris that, though. I'd die rather than have him think I'm hinting.

Anyway, he said he didn't like the outfit. He told me I'm too pretty to be dressing like that. That I'd attract the wrong kind of attention. He kept looking at my legs, but it didn't feel as good as the time I'd had on my hip-huggers and platform shoes and I'd caught him looking at me. Twice. He'd smiled then.

Today he just frowned. And watched other guys watching me.

I threw the skirt away as soon as I got home.

CHAPTER THREE

January 28, 1977

Today's Friday. I haven't seen or talked to Chris for two days. I needed him so badly last night. Dad's been having chest pains. And they said that the arteries to his heart are hardening. He might have to go on oxygen at night sometimes. He's only sixty-two. Mom looked kind of scared, with those pinched creases around her mouth that mean she's holding stuff in.

Even after forty years of marriage, they're as much in love as schoolkids, holding hands, kissing. If one of them goes, the other will, too. I just know it.

They both acted like everything was fine. And maybe it will be. There's some new medication that slows down hardening of the arteries. And the doctor talked about surgery if things get really bad.

But when they left for choir practice, I walked around the house and cried. I picked up the phone to call Chris, but then I thought of him standing in the store the other day, pretending he didn't find my outfit attractive, and I wondered what was the use.

If he wants to pretend there's nothing between us, that's his choice. I certainly can't force him to love me. I don't even want to.

I want a man to love me like my father loves my mother. Openly and without shame.

I talked to Val for a bit. While we were on the phone her youngest sister—you know, the four-year-old, Kristy—called out to her and when Val said, "Just a sec," Kristy shouted, "No more secs" at the top of her lungs. Val's mom thought she said sex and came running. I could hear it all happening and I laughed so hard I almost started crying again. I love Val. She's the best friend a girl could have.

I was going to tell her about Dad, but by that time I was feeling so much better, I didn't want to get all bummed out again. We made plans to go to the mall tomorrow.

We were still laughing about Kristy when we hung up. And then when I went to bed I started to worry if Mom's heart would go bad, too. She'll be sixty in a couple of years. That sounds so old to me now.

Brett Fry asked me to go see *Rocky* tonight. Such a stupid boy thing, to ask a girl to a boxing movie on their first date, but I'd actually like to see this one. Seems all the kids at school saw it over Christmas break and everyone's talking about it. Even Val. She saw it with her brothers and sisters and said it was the best romance ever.

But I'm not in the mood for a romance tonight.

And I couldn't bear the thought of going out with another guy. Not even Brett Fry, who I had a crush on my whole sophomore and junior years. I look at him now and wonder why I thought he was such a hunk.

Anyway, I'm still freaked out about Dad. So I just wanted to stay close to home tonight. I wish Chris would call, but I know he won't. He's never called me.

I'm not going to call him anymore, either. Contrary to what he might think, I'm not some little schoolgirl with a crush. And I don't chase guys. Even when I'm sure he's the love of my life.

So, Dear Diary, it might be just me and you for a while. I'm glad you're here. Some nights I don't know what I'd do without you.

February 13, 2008, 4:45 p.m.

MONICA TOLD HERSELF that it was only because she hadn't been sleeping well that she had to wipe tears from her eyes before she could go on. She always got weepy when she was tired.

The tears had nothing to do with her understanding her mother's pain. Nothing to do with Shane's insistence that he knew what was best for her future happiness—a life without him and impotence.

Like sex was important to her.

Making *love* was important—and something they could do in various ways every single day, even if Shane's condition turned out to be more than temporary.

But like Chris with Carol, Shane was being stubborn and domineering in his insistence that Monica didn't know her own mind as well as he did. That she couldn't see into the future like he could. He'd moved out. Was filing for divorce—to set her free.

And if at some point he became a fully functioning male again—as he put it—and she was unattached, they could try a second time.

Like Chris with Carol, Shane was leaving her no choice but to carry on. Alone.

But unlike Carol, Monica didn't have a Dear Diary to turn to for comfort.

January 31, 1977

Oh, Dearest Diary, I'm so confused! Why don't they tell you that love really isn't a splendid thing? It hurts and it makes you crazy and drives you to do things you promise yourself you aren't going to do.

I spent the whole weekend convincing myself that I was over Chris. He was a fluke. A ship in the night. Someone I once knew. I'm not going to be a fool. Or make a fool of myself over him.

I can't make him accept me in his life, no matter how much I believe our connection is forever.

But I can't resist him, even for sixty seconds. After all my decisions and talking to myself this weekend, when he came into the store today I couldn't look away. I was only scheduled from five to seven because of the meeting with a rep from the University of Wisconsin—Dad's alma mater—and Chris always comes in around four, while his mother naps before dinner.

I thought I was safe.

And then there he was. Standing at my register, buying a pack of mints. Nothing else. No medicine. Nothing.

It was obvious, Dear Diary, that he was there to see me.

I can hear his voice now. Can remember every single word he said.

"How are you?"

"Fine." I wasn't lying. I *was* fine. I'd moved on.

And then he lowered his head like he does, his brown eyes reaching into mine, and said, "You sure?"

And I went and got all stupid and started to cry. I couldn't speak. Just nodded. Thank goodness there were no other customers in line. Kind of odd how the whole store was deserted right then.

I don't know if that was a good thing or not.

"I was getting worried about you."

My heart began to pound when he said those words. You should've heard the tone of his voice. It was all warm and soft and deep. And his eyes…I kid you not, I could've melted in them.

I guess my heart did.

"Why?" I asked him, shocked that I could even get a word out, my throat was so tight.

He shrugged like he wanted to look all casual

and nonchalant, but he'd already given himself away. The pack of mints did that.

"I haven't heard from you in a few days," he said. I stared at him. "And then when I came in today and you weren't here…"

I knew it, Dear Diary! He'd already been in today. He'd come back just to see me.

You tell me, how could I resist that?

I have no idea how I managed it, but somehow I was able to keep looking him straight in the eye and say, "I was beginning to feel like a pest."

He frowned, like he truly had no idea what I was talking about. "Why?"

"Calling you all the time."

"I look forward to those calls."

"But you won't call me."

"It's not appropriate."

"Well, maybe it's not appropriate for me to call you, either."

I had him there, Diary. I could see it in the drop of his shoulders and the way his mouth got straight.

I couldn't believe what happened next. I expected him to make some innocuous comment and tell me to have a good day and leave. To tell me that he'd see me the next time he was in.

I was all prepared to tell him that no, he wouldn't. I'd switch my schedule if I had to. Quit my job even. But I couldn't keep pretending.

I didn't get a chance to say any of that.

"What do you want from me?" His question was so sincere, the thoughts just ran out of my head.

And then, before I could start to think again, I opened my mouth. "I want you to acknowledge that we care about each other. That it isn't just me who feels this…whatever it is…between us."

He didn't say anything for the longest time. I was getting worried that if he didn't hurry up, someone was going to come in and interrupt us before we could get through the most crucial moment of my life.

"I'm ten years older than you," he said.

I hate those words, Diary. I really, really hate them. "So?"

"I'm a high school teacher and you're a senior."

"You aren't teaching now. And you don't teach at my school. And I'm going to be graduating in a few months anyway."

His eyes narrowed and he stared at me some more. I wish I'd had on something a little cuter than the old jeans and sweater I'd worn because they were comfortable and because who really cared how I looked anymore?

"Have you told your parents about us?"

He'd asked me that before. He didn't understand that I didn't tell my parents a lot of things. He didn't know about my dad's recent health news.

"No."

I could see how disappointed he was and started to explain but before I got any words out he held up his hand.

"Call me when you do."

Without so much as looking at me again, he turned and walked out. I watched him all the way down the block but he didn't glance back even once.

CHAPTER FOUR

February 2, 1977

Dearest Diary,

I told them. I didn't want to. Didn't feel it was the best way to handle this situation. I'm eighteen and within my legal rights to have whatever relationships I choose to have. But I couldn't sleep last night thinking about the determination in Chris's eyes.

He said he looked forward to my calls and the idea that I was denying him that brief respite during these hard times, while his mother's slowly dying, clawed at my heart.

Mom and Dad forbade me to see him or speak to him ever again. I'm sure they would've forbidden me to think of him, too, if they'd been able to figure out how to do it.

They made it sound like he's a pervert. They don't know him or anything about him. And yet they're certain their judgment is sound.

And that mine, because I've never had a boyfriend before, is not.

I love my parents, Dearest Diary. Incredibly much. But I cannot just arbitrarily accept this erroneous decision. Particularly when it involves the rest of my life.

They're the ones who've always warned me about the dangers of following the crowd. They taught me to think for myself.

Remember that time I went to church camp with Sheila and the people there told me Mom and Dad weren't saved because they didn't go to Sheila's church? I called them crying and hysterical, sure they were going to burn in hell and begged them to come and get me. I expected them to be as scared as I was. Instead, they very calmly told me to question what I was being told. To think about who I knew God to be. And then to figure out for myself if he would exact such payment.

They never did tell me what they thought about the church's edict, or their own salvation.

I ended up staying the whole week at that camp. I helped with a service project, making little outfits for premature babies in a Third World country. That was the first time I learned about loving people who weren't close to me, people I didn't even know, and it changed my life. And I determined for myself which religious teachings were true for me.

Remember how, when Sheila found out I wasn't

going to be "saved," she no longer wanted to hang out with me?

That hurt a lot, for a while. But I was glad I'd decided for myself what was right and true.

Which is why I can't let Mom and Dad tell me what to think now.

Tonight, they said that as long as I live in their house, I have to live under their rules and that means no contact with Chris.

They *could* kick me out, I suppose, but they aren't going to do that. They need me. I mow the grass and do the shoveling. Ever since Mom tripped and broke her ankle last year, leading to the discovery of her severe osteoporosis, I do most of the cleaning and I bring in the groceries, too, now that Dad's back has gotten so bad.

Still, if they did kick me out (they're going to have to hire someone to do that stuff when I leave for college in the fall, anyway) Chris would let me put a sleeping bag on the floor at his place. I could help him take care of his mom, give him some relief. I've had some experience with bedpans and things like that. Mom was flat on her back for almost six weeks last year with that ankle problem. After her surgery, she'd had to keep it elevated twenty-four hours a day.

Anyway, Diary, I'm rambling again. Sorry. You know I have a tendency to do that when I'm upset.

I haven't called Chris yet. I'm not sure what to say. I'll have to tell him my parents weren't happy. I can't lie to him. But if I tell him quite how badly they took the news, he'll run for sure.

I can't let that happen.

February 13, 2008, 5:15 p.m.

SHE HADN'T WANTED to tell Shane about the doctor's call. About the possibility that the problems he'd been having could be permanent. They'd never had secrets between them. But Shane was such a man's man in that area. Probably more so because he'd been raised solely by his father (as she had, which had given them something in common from the start) and the elder Mr. Slater had pushed his son to excel in all things masculine. From sports to women to baby-making.

Still, he'd changed so much since their first date in college. Become the man he'd said he wanted to be. Still strong, both emotionally and physically, but gentler, too. He'd said her love had changed him.

She'd gambled on that. Told him that the doctor said his inability to maintain an erection long enough to have an orgasm could be a result of his adult-onset diabetes.

She'd gambled and lost. Her marriage. Her life. *Him.*

February 3, 1977

Dear Diary,
Is there ever a time when life gets easier? Even a little bit? Must it always demand such painful prices for the things we want?

I called Chris from a pay phone this afternoon. I wanted to talk to him in private without worrying that Mom or Dad would come walking in. I'm all paranoid now that they're going to be watching my every move, even though I've never once given them cause not to trust me.

Is that why I'm paranoid? Because now I *am* giving them cause?

Doesn't really matter at this point, I guess.

I knew Chris would be coming into the store tomorrow to get his mother's heparin injections and I had to let him know I'd told them before I saw him again.

Or worse, before he avoided seeing me.

And I couldn't leave him hanging, waiting for a call.

So I phoned him. I squirmed through his questions, letting him know that my parents weren't happy, but that was all. I asked him to give them time.

I didn't tell him they forbade any contact between the two of us. And I should have. I see that now.

I guess that's what they mean about hindsight being twenty-twenty.

If I'd had any hint of what Chris was going to do…

He called them, Dear Diary. Can you believe it? Every time I think about it I want to die. I play the conversation over and over in my head, guessing how it must have gone, filling in the blanks with the things

I did know—the things I heard from my father's side of the conversation. And I get hot with shame. And embarrassment. I feel so hopeless. And helpless.

They're all talking about me as though I'm an imbecile or a child, unable to form my own thoughts, know my own feelings, make my own decisions.

As if I wasn't there. As if my life wasn't my own. As if I can't be trusted with the life that God gave me.

Chris will probably never like my parents now. And I can't say I blame him. He has no idea what great people they normally are.

Dad called him some terrible names that I can't even write here and threatened to have him arrested and charged with sexual misconduct with a minor if he so much as stepped foot in the drugstore again. Chris could fight the charges, and maybe win, since he's never even touched me—let alone had "misconduct" with me back in October and November, when I was still seventeen. But just the charges could lose him, a schoolteacher, his entire career.

Even I know that much.

Chris tried to tell them we'd never done more than talk. He told them he has only the best of intentions. And that he was planning to wait until I was older before he pursued anything else with me. He told them he only wanted their permission to speak with me on the phone occasionally. (I heard Dad tell Mom that one.)

They threatened to call his high school in Tennessee if he spoke one word to me on the phone or by any other means.

And then they told him I was grounded. I would be quitting my job, finishing my education at home and losing my car. They said they were going to take the phone out of my room and that they'd be monitoring every single conversation I had, every move I made.

It's ridiculous, Diary. There's no way they can do that. I've never, ever seen them act so crazy. It was like I didn't even know them. But they wouldn't back down.

Later, after Chris had hung up, Mom and Dad and I got in the first yelling match we'd ever had. I couldn't believe it. I heard myself screaming at my parents, saw the shock on their faces and wondered what had happened to me.

I told them I refused to miss out on my last few months at school. Nor was I quitting my job. They could take my phone out of my room. What do I care? Chris probably won't ever speak to me again, anyway.

They still say I'm grounded. That I'm not allowed to drive or go anywhere for the next four months—until graduation.

I'm sorry, but I'm eighteen now and I'll be coming and going as I see fit.

I would've told them that, too, except Dad got all gray and pasty-looking and we just stopped yelling as quickly as we'd started. We didn't mention Chris again all night.

I'm dying inside, Diary. Dying at the thought of never seeing Chris again. Never talking to him.

Dying at the thought of having my mother so upset with me. Of losing my dad.

Just dying.

CHAPTER FIVE

February 4, 1977

Oh my gosh. I tell you, Dearest, Dearest Diary, I sure didn't expect today. I have no idea what to make of it.

Things are horrible with Mom and Dad. It's never been like this. *Ever.* They aren't just mad at me. Or upset. They're like cold, heartless guards over a death-row criminal. The entire conversation at dinner was them grilling me about my day. They practically asked how many times I went to the bathroom. They wanted me to account for every single second.

Trust has always been the mainstay for me and them, and Mom and Dad with each other. I just don't get why everything's gone so wrong. But I'm telling you, Diary, I can't go on like this.

Maybe I won't have to. Maybe I'll just move out now, before I graduate, start my own life, and maybe then they'll love me again. Once I'm away, married, they'll see that I'm responsible. That I can be trusted.

They'll treat me like an adult instead of an ignorant child.

Surely, when I present them with their first grandchild, they'll open their arms to me again. Mom loves babies. So does Dad. They both wanted a huge family and had to try for more than twenty years before they had me.

I've heard the story so many times....

"You were an angel sent from heaven to your daddy and me," Mom used to say. I know the story by heart but never tire of hearing Mom tell it. Or watching the bemused expression on Dad's face when she does. *"It was May 10, 1958. I'd been out in the garden, weeding, and when I stood up, I almost passed out. It was a balmy day, not too hot, and the sun was shining nicely. I'd had my normal bowl of oatmeal for breakfast. And a banana. Nothing that should've upset my stomach. But suddenly I was so sick I didn't think I was going to make it inside. Somehow I did. And into the bathroom. And that's where Billy found me when he got home from work that afternoon— lying asleep on the bathroom floor."*

Billy. My dad. I always get all warm inside when I hear Mom call him by that name. No one else would dare. He's always Bill. Or William. But anytime they're fooling around or tender or emotional, he's Billy. And every time she tells this story.

"I could see the fear in Billy's eyes when he gathered me up and carried me the two blocks to my doctor's office. He kept telling me everything

*was going to be fine. I didn't believe him. I knew
something inside me was very, very wrong....*

"*Sitting in the doctor's office, all I could think
about, all I could see, was Billy. I couldn't leave him
yet. I was only forty years old. He needed me. I
couldn't break his heart that way. Somehow I'd
find the strength to battle whatever was wrong.*"

Just as I'm going to find the strength to fight for
Chris, Dearest Diary. And win. I can't break his
heart, either.

But can I finish telling you the story? It makes me
feel so good to remember it—makes me feel like
Mom and Dad will always love me, no matter what...

"'*Martha? Billy?' Doctor Arnold had an odd look
on his face as he peered at us over his glasses,
calling us back into his office. Clara, his nurse,
was nowhere to be seen. That, more than anything,
told me the news was bad.*

"'*What is it, Doc?' Billy's voice shook, his hand
shook, as he held mine.*"

Dad always holds Mom's hand during this part
of the story.

"'*I don't quite believe it myself,' Doc said, frown-
ing. 'I've heard of it, of course, but never seen it
happen....'*

"*Oh, it was bad. Fear went clear through me. But
I would fight it. Whatever it was. I gave Billy's hand
a squeeze, letting him know I wasn't giving up. I
wasn't leaving him.*

"'*I've looked at the test twice,' the doctor said.*

'And based on everything else you've told me, I can draw no other conclusion....'

"'How long has she got?' Billy's voice was tense.

"'I'd say about six months. Give or take a week or so. I'm putting November 10th as your due date.'

"Date? They gave you an actual date when you could expect to die?

"'Due date?' Billy asked, just as confused as I was.

"'Why, yes,' Dr. Arnold said. 'We did the blood and urine tests, talked about missed periods....'

"What? I'd thought they were going through standard procedures to find out what was and was not working in my body. Looking for symptoms. For...

"'Are you saying—' I couldn't finish. Couldn't swallow. I stared at the doctor, my hand in Billy's cold and clammy.

"'You're pregnant, Martha. You're going to have a baby.'

"'I'm forty years old, Doctor. I can't have a baby.'

"The doctor nodded, his spectacles sliding a little farther down his nose. 'That's what I assumed, too, though, of course, I've read about many women your age and older giving birth. It's just not something you see every day. But I checked twice and everything else adds up. We'll do an internal examination. You can schedule that for next week. But I'm sure that's what we're dealing with here.'

"'She's not sick.' Billy's voice was blank. The look on his face dazed.

"'No, Billy, she's not sick.'

"It wasn't until Dr.Arnold broke out into a grin, that the truth started to dawn on me.

"'Congratulations, you two, you're going to be a mama and daddy.'

"That was when I remembered Valentine's Day. Billy. Loving me."

Valentine's Day. I was conceived on Valentine's Day, Diary. I don't think I've ever told you that, either. That's just ten days from now.

Oh, Diary, how could something so great have gone so wrong?

I went to work today, fully expecting my mom or dad to be there, intending to watch me the entire time. I was right; Mom *was* there. And then, an hour later, Dad came.

They don't trust me at all.

If Chris came by, I didn't hear. He stayed away from me. I'm guessing he picked up the heparin injections while I was still in school.

But what Mom and Dad don't know is that Chris didn't run. He didn't turn his back on me….

February 13, 2008, 5:45 p.m.

GOOD FOR YOU, DADDY, Monica thought, wiping away a fresh spate of tears. Shane, on hearing the doctor's prognosis, had done exactly the opposite of what her father had done. He'd left.

Oh, he'd called her several hours later to come and

get him. He'd drunk himself into such a stupor he'd been unable to get himself home.

But he'd left again. A week later. Two days after Christmas. And hadn't been back since. Monica turned back to the entry she'd been reading. The longest to date. So long her mother had dated it a second time as she'd turned to a new page.

February 4, 1977

I still can't believe it. Chris hasn't been scared off. And yet, inside my deepest heart, I'm not the least bit surprised. Because my heart recognized Chris from the moment we met back in September, when he'd first come to Chicago with his mother for tests. All last fall, throughout his mother's scary test results, a horrible Thanksgiving and sad Christmas holiday, I was compelled to comfort Chris. And received so much from him, as well.

He's so like my parents, if only they realized it. He encourages me to strive to be my best self. Not to settle for less. To believe in myself. He bought me a Raggedy Ann doll for Christmas because I'd told him I'd never played with dolls. He sent taxis to pick me up from school and take me to work when the weather was below zero.

And never once, in all those months, did he so much as shake my hand.

He still hasn't. But he actually came to the house. Just a little while ago. Even though it was barely after nine, Mom and Dad were already in bed and neither of us wanted to wake them.

He was outside the enclosed front porch, standing there in the dark. I didn't open the screen door that would allow him access to the porch. And the front door. But, God, how I wished I could.

I stood at the door staring at him. I wanted to pull him inside, into my arms. To hug him and kiss him and never let go.

And then I wanted to show him my house. The place where I've lived my entire life. My space. All my things. The pictures of me and my parents on the mantel. The misshapen ceramic ashtray I made for my dad when I was in kindergarten. My room.

I didn't, of course. He wouldn't have come in. Not without my parents' approval. But neither did he just leave.

For a few minutes he just studied me, as though he was seeing me for the very first time. Like he was making sure I was the same girl as the one behind the register at the drugstore.

And then his eyes got really deep and glistening. His mouth opened and I thought he was going to say something, but he didn't.

"What?" I finally asked. I couldn't stand it anymore. I had to know what his eyes were hiding. What his heart was feeling.

"You have nothing to be ashamed of," he said.

I wasn't sure about that. I'd only been thinking of myself the day before when I'd pushed my father practically to the point of a heart attack. I'd upset the two people who'd cared for my every need for all of my almost eighteen years.

"You have a generous heart, Carol. You're strong and honest and open and not afraid to reach out for what you want."

He was telling me something important. Far more important than the usual believe-in-yourself talks he gave me.

"We care for each other in a way most people haven't experienced. Whether we see each other or not, whether we even touch, we each know the other is out there. And that knowledge comforts us."

Oh, God, my Dear Diary, he was so right. And it felt so good to hear him say out loud what I've known for so long. Such a relief to have the deepest yearnings of my heart spoken aloud.

"Yes," I said, because he seemed to be waiting for a response and I couldn't come up with anything more coherent than that.

"They can't treat you like this, Carol. They're locking you up, shoving you into a corner, and you've done absolutely nothing wrong. You were honest. Never so much as had coffee with me behind their backs. You've never done *anything* to betray their trust."

"I know." But I also know that Mom and Dad and I, we're different. It's always seemed like the three of us against the world. And now, out of the blue, I've brought a fourth into our midst. Without warning.

Someone they don't know. Didn't pick for me. I didn't ask them before falling in love with Chris.

And he's ten years older than I am.

I understand their concern.

But not their lack of trust.

"I'm coming back tomorrow," Chris said then, speaking softly. He was standing upright, his shoulders big and broad in the tan suede winter coat I'd first seen him wear the day before Thanksgiving. His once-short dark hair was now touching the collar of the coat.

"I don't think that's a good idea," I said, shivering. From the cold coming through the screen, I told myself, but I knew it was more.

"I'm not going to allow their threats to make me turn my back on you, Carol. Not after all the months of support and caring you've given me. Even when I've offered you no encouragement, you've been there, believing in our friendship. Fighting for it. It's time for me to do the same for you."

My whole body melted at his words. I could feel tears forming in the back of my throat, behind my eyes. I was afraid my voice would wobble if I tried to speak but I had to say it. "You could lose your job. You don't have to do this."

"You want us never to see each other again? Never speak again?"

"No."

"Then there's no other alternative."

"They don't have to know about it." I hated even saying the words. They were so much against my heart's way of living. Not telling my parents about something I felt I had every right and ability to decide on my own was one thing. Deliberately lying to them was another.

"I'm not doing that to you," Chris said immediately. "I will not compromise you."

And that, Dear Diary, is when I fell irrevocably head over heels in love, forever in love, with Christopher Warren.

CHAPTER SIX

February 5, 1977

I'm writing this in the bathroom, Dear Diary. My parents went through my room today after Chris left, confiscating anything they thought might prove there was something going on between him and me. I sat there with tears streaming down my face, promising them that nothing had happened, that they weren't going to find a thing.

And I hid you, just in case. I couldn't survive if they got hold of you, read you, exposed you to a court system and managed to put Chris in jail because of a young and stupid girl's ramblings.

I couldn't bear to lose you. You are my life. Maybe my sanity.

I cried until I couldn't breathe, but it didn't make any difference. They didn't soften at all. It was the first time I've ever cried in front of my mother without her putting her arms around me.

Life is changing. Fast.

I'm scared, Diary. Not of Chris. Or even of loving him. But of life. Of losing my parents. My safe refuge from the world.

What if I'm no good at love? What if I let Chris down? Disappoint him? What if, when we finally manage to have real time together, we find out that I really am too young, too immature for him?

He told Mom and Dad he was going to call me. That he intended to ask me out.

They told him that if he did, they'd expose the fact that he'd begun a relationship with me while I was still a minor. A high school student. Dad had phone records proving I'd called Chris and that we'd talked for more than an hour on several occasions in the past months.

They said they'd talked to my boss, who could testify that I spent many of my breaks with Chris, starting in September, often walking out back where we could be alone.

It didn't matter that Chris and I both told them that all we'd done was talk. Usually about his mother. Or school.

I'd told him about a manager at the store who'd come on to me. Chris's suggestions had not only ended the inappropriate behavior, but lost the man his job.

My parents weren't swayed, even then. Can you believe it, Diary? Even when they heard that Chris had come to my aid, saved me from possible sexual abuse.

So it's a standoff. I'm sitting here shaking. Chris knows Tuesday is my day off. Will he call?

Will he ever call?

And what if he does?

Will my parents really hate me? Enough to ruin the life of the man I love, simply because he loves me back? Can I let him take that risk?

I don't know, Dear Diary.

I just don't know.

February 6, 1977

I haven't heard from Chris today. Mom and Dad question every move I make. They watch me constantly.

No one is happy.

February 7, 1977

No word from Chris. Mom surprised me with tickets to the dinner theater tomorrow night. My evening off work. Val's invited.

It'll be the four of us.

Mom hasn't smiled in days. But she's pretending this is a happy occasion, something fun for us all to share. She's pretending she bought the tickets on a whim, but I know differently. She bought them so I wouldn't be free to see Chris.

She can't possibly think she'll be able to occupy my time every single day I have off for the rest of my life.

February 8, 1977 (morning)

Dear Diary, I know I don't normally bother you in the morning, but I had to talk to you. My stomach is a mass of nerves. I hardly slept all night. Dozed for a few minutes and then would wake again.

It's Tuesday and if I don't hear from Chris today, my day off, I'm not going to. I just know it.

Being in love, coupled with my parents' withdrawal, is horrible. Lonely.

I'm worried sick.

What if Chris calls? Do I spare him the trouble my parents have threatened? Or do I stand beside him and fight for us?

What if he doesn't call?

I've been waiting for this day for months. And now that it's here I don't feel ready for it.

One way or another, today is going to mark my entire future.

February 8, 1977 (night)

It happened. Just as we were leaving to go pick up Val for the dinner theater the phone rang. Mom and Dad had bought me a new red plaid long skirt and jacket with a silk blouse and matching shoes and purse, and I dropped the new purse, spilling lipstick and keys and everything on the floor. Mom looked at my stuff lying there and then answered the phone.

I don't know what Chris said, but I knew it was him.

Mom just hung up.

When the phone rang a second time, I reached for it, pulling it away from my mom.

She didn't try to stop me. I was on my own.

I didn't want to be.

Mom and Dad were standing there watching me. My new purse was on the floor at their feet. They were all dressed up and had actually been smiling as we'd headed for the door.

Now they both looked old to me. Old and pinched and angry.

I couldn't bear that they weren't on my side. Supporting me.

And then I heard his voice. "Hello" was all it took and I knew I was doing the right thing. That I had to fight for Chris.

My heart could see what I could not. It could see beyond the moment and into the future. It knew what I was on earth to accomplish. And what I needed to help me through.

We only talked for a few seconds and I remember every single word.

"Are you free tonight?" I'd imagined the words a hundred times that day, but never with that low, intimate note of affection.

"No. We're on our way to the theater. Mom got the tickets at the last minute."

I held my breath waiting to see what he'd do with that information.

"Would you like to have dinner tomorrow when you get off work?"

Air came out of my lungs in a whoosh. "What about your mother?" I asked.

"I've got a nurse coming to sit with her."

This was it, then. Mom and Dad seemed to be staring a hole in my back. I couldn't see them, but I knew that's what they were doing. I could feel them.

And I had to choose. Chris or my parents. A man I'd only known for a few months, a man I'd never shared anything with but conversation? Or the two people who'd been there for me my entire life, loving me, supporting me, protecting me?

Oh, Diary, my heart breaks again as I tell you about it. How did I get into this position? I never meant to hurt anyone.

Well, you know what I did, don't you? You already know the words I said.

I said, "I'd love to have dinner with you." Of course.

Dad's chin dropped to his chest. A man defeated. Mom started to cry.

And we went to the theater.

February 10, 1977

Oh, Dearest Diary! I feel so… I just… How can I possibly feel so incredibly, perfectly great, and so horribly sad at the same time? I've gone out with Chris three times in two days. I can't talk long, Diary. I'm so exhausted I can hardly keep my eyes open.

But I needed to tell you that being with Chris

is everything I knew it would be, and so much more. I'm at peace when I'm with him. It doesn't matter if we're sitting at the diner down the street from the drugstore, drinking hot chocolate and talking for the two hours he has, or walking by the lake or grocery shopping for his mother. That's all we've done. Nothing big and romantic and exciting, because right now his first priority has to be his mother. And yet, I've never felt so magical in my life.

Tomorrow I'm going to meet his mother. We're going to have dinner with her. I'm so nervous I feel like throwing up. I hope I can manage to eat when I'm there. We're having baked spaghetti. Apparently it's Chris's specialty and his mother loves it. She used to make it when he and his sister were little.

Mom and Dad were already in bed last night and again tonight when I got home. I stopped in to tell them good-night, but they were both asleep. Either for real or pretending, I'm not sure.

I miss them so much, Diary. I cried myself to sleep last night. I wish they could see Chris for what he really is. I wish they could see into his heart—and mine. They have nothing to worry about. I know what I'm doing. I know Chris is the man for me. It's crazy, and I know that, too. But Mom and Dad are the ones who taught me that you can't predict or control life. When it happens, it happens. You have to recognize it. And then have the courage to live it.

I just have to believe they'll come around.

And in the meantime… I hope Chris kisses me soon. I'm dying to feel his lips against mine. To be held against his body. The wait is killing me.

February 13, 2008, 6:04 p.m.

IT HAD BEEN ALMOST six weeks since Shane had kissed Monica. But not since he'd kissed a woman. It was no more than five days since he'd done that. She'd had light brown hair with those auburn highlights everyone knew were fake.

She'd been perfectly made-up, too. And her clothes…

As she'd been doing for five days, Monica tried to push the vision away. Tried not to see the tight black slacks next to her husband's bar stool at the upscale club near their house. She didn't want to know that the woman had perfectly manicured red nails, nor that they'd run familiarly through Shane's blond hair, as though it hadn't been the first time….

Didn't want to remember the black leather and fur jacket, the nicely sized rounded breasts, the husky chuckle just before Shane had lowered his head to the stranger's lips. He'd lingered there, tasting her.

Who knew how long the kiss would've gone on, or where it would've led, if Shane hadn't opened his eyes and seen Monica standing there?

She'd gone to the club, one of their favorite spots, specifically to look for him the previous Friday. To tell him enough was enough. To come home. And if her tough-girl attitude hadn't worked, she'd been prepared to beg.

Instead, she'd embarrassed herself with an open mouth and tears in her eyes as she'd run out, ignoring his voice behind her.

Even in high-heeled boots, Monica had run farther, faster, making it to her car before Shane could catch up with her. She'd had the advantage, of course. She'd been closer to the door. And hadn't needed to make excuses to anyone before dashing out.

He'd reached her as she was about to drive off. Monica could still see his face gazing in at her.

"Monica. Honey. Please open the door."

His brow was creased, his eyes wide, imploring. "Come on, sweetie. I'm begging you."

Apparently he'd been prepared to beg, too. But for Monica five days ago, it had been too little too late.

She'd driven away with him still standing in the street. If he hadn't jumped back, she might have run over his toes.

She'd refused to answer his calls ever since. And the door, too, when he'd come pounding both Saturday and Sunday.

Shane Slater was out of her life. Period. Decision made.

Just as Carol's had been that weekend after Chris's negative reaction to her miniskirt?

Was she *really* through with Shane? she asked herself now. Could she be if she was still considering tomorrow's appointment at the fertility clinic?

If she was so sure she wasn't going to go, why hadn't she canceled? What was she waiting for?

Or was it more a case of knowing that Shane was the one great love of her life? The same way Carol had known… Even with the marriage over, there would be no other men for her. And she wanted children.

So why not Shane's?

CHAPTER SEVEN

February 13, 1977

Hi. Sorry I haven't written lately. It's been a rough few days.

My dad had a heart attack, Diary. I still can't believe it. It happened Friday morning. I think. My days are all running together. But it must've been because I was getting ready for school. He's still in the hospital. In the cardiac ward. He has to have open heart surgery, Diary, or he's going to die. They've scheduled it for tomorrow. Valentine's Day. Mom and I have to be at the hospital by seven so we can see him before he goes in. The surgery could take anywhere from two to seven hours, depending on exactly what they find.

He's got the best team of doctors in Chicago. They've had many successes at this type of operation. At sixty-two Dad's an excellent candidate, and he doesn't smoke or drink so his prognosis is good.

But they're going to saw his chest in half!

And they're only giving him a sixty percent chance.

I feel so responsible, Diary. Like this is my fault for pushing them about Chris. And yet, I need him now more than ever.

He's been a rock through all of this. I've had to be strong for Mom. I'm the one running around getting doctors to talk to us. Driving her to and from the hospital. Making sure she's eating.

And Chris is being strong for me. His apartment is a couple of blocks from the hospital and he's walked over several times. Even met me in the cafeteria for a cup of hot chocolate last night while Mom had some time alone with Dad.

I think she knows I'm seeing him, but she hasn't said anything.

He's going to be in and out all day tomorrow. He says he won't come into the family waiting room because he doesn't want to further upset my mom, but he can't just leave me there alone, either. We're going to meet every two hours down by the elevator. And if I'm able to go to the cafeteria, we will.

Knowing he's going to be there is the only thing keeping me sane right now.

I never did meet his mother, but he said she sends her good wishes and is keeping us in her prayers.

That's very kind.

February 14, 1977

It's three in the morning, Dearest Diary. I left you just an hour ago, but I can't sleep. I'm so worried about my father I can't rest. Can't find any calm at all.

What if something happens to him tomorrow? What if tonight is his last night on earth? I should be there with him. Mom should be there. Not some strangers walking in and out of his room. He shouldn't be alone. We love him so much.

I love him so much.

They made us go home. Said we needed our rest, and that he did, too.

Tomorrow night, if all goes well, Mom can stay with him. We've already arranged to have a bed moved into the little room off the ICU. It was the only way I could get Mom to come home tonight.

That, and Dad telling her to leave.

He was fully conscious this evening. And bossing us around. He told me to call the school to get my homework. And to put out the trash cans in the morning so the neighbor's cats don't get into them. He told me to drive carefully. To make sure my mother gets some rest. He told us both to eat.

And he asked her to bring his robe when we visit in the morning. He hates the hospital attire.

He didn't say anything about Chris. Didn't ask anything. I didn't mention him, either.

Diary, what if I caused this? What if my insisting on seeing Chris was what made this happen?

Sorry about that blotch there. I can't seem to stop crying tonight. I love my daddy so much. He's been good to me every day of my life. No matter how tired he was when he came in from the press machines at the *Chicago Tribune*, he'd always take time for me. He'd ask about my day. And listen while I rambled on about unimportant little-girl stuff. When I went out for softball in junior high, he spent hours in the yard playing catch with me. And when I made the cheerleading squad in freshman year, he was at every single game. He taught me to bowl and to swim and how to shoot a rifle.

Yeah, there were times when it seemed he was being a little tough on me, grounding me for a week for talking back to my mother, and for a month when I stole a Tootsie Roll from the drugstore where I now work. But I always knew he loved me. Always.

I can't imagine life without him.

I'm not ready to lose him. To lose either of them. I know it's going to happen sometime. Sooner than it will for a lot of my friends.

This is where being an only child sucks canal water.

And being the only child of older parents—even more.

Hold on a sec…I have to get a tissue.

Okay, sorry. I'm back.

I'm probably being a baby. But I *can't* lose them yet, Diary. There's still so much to share with them. So much for them to teach me. For my daddy to teach me. Holidays to share. Presents to buy for them. Things I still want to do for them, to show them how much I love them.

Daddy has to walk me down the aisle.

And hold my children in his arms.

He has to see me graduate from high school. And the University of Wisconsin.

He can't leave me yet, Diary. He just can't.

I'm only eighteen.

February 13, 2008, 6:13 p.m.

MAYBE SHE SHOULD call Shane. Life was too short for hurt feelings and insecurities to get in the way of a love as deep and strong as hers and Shane's. Shane was a good man, last Friday night—and any other times he'd been with another woman—notwithstanding.

She remembered the week her dad died. Shane had driven down to Tennessee with her. Sat with her. Listened. Laughed as she relived childhood memories. Held her hand when the doctors told her that in spite of their best efforts they couldn't save him.

Shane had been her strength then.

If she even considered keeping the clinic appointment and attempting to have his child, she should call him.

CHAPTER EIGHT

February 14, 1977 (more)

It's six now. I've been up since five, showered and ready to go. We have to leave in half an hour.

There were no calls from the hospital during the night. It's only been three days, but listening for that phone call all night, and feeling relieved in the morning that it didn't come, seems like a way of life to me.

Being at the hospital all day, talking to my mom, trying to find pieces for the puzzle we've kind of been working on in the small waiting room two doors away from Dad's, seeing Chris, cataloging Dad's features every time I'm allowed in to see him, trying to determine if his color is better or worse, if his breathing has improved, watching the little lines squiggle across the screen beside his bed, holding my breath—it seems as if this is the only life I've ever known.

Last week, school, eating dinner at the table, the fight about Chris, they all seem like a very distant and faded movie I once saw.

There is nothing but this. Nothing but knowing that my father could die. Nothing but spending every ounce of my energy on keeping him alive.

Sorry for the messy writing. My hand's a little shaky.

I don't know how Chris is doing it. How he can spend all day every day watching his mother die. They aren't even trying to cure her anymore. They're just doing what they can to give her a few more months. And to make sure she's comfortable.

Not that I wouldn't do exactly the same thing. If they can give me even a few more months with Daddy, I'll take them, spend every moment I can right there beside him. I just don't know how my heart's going to get through this without breaking into a million pieces. I don't know how I'll survive. I can hardly breathe for thinking about the day to come.

Valentine's Day.

A day for love.

Please, God, let my love for my father be enough to keep him here on earth with us. Let Mom's love be enough.

We need him.

You got that?

We need him.

Mom's calling me. I gotta go….

8:30 a.m.

I'm in the bathroom now. It's big. A private room off the waiting room we're in today. On a different floor.

Where the operating rooms are. I guess they put all of us with potential deaths on our hands in separate places from the regular people.

No kids are allowed up here. I wonder if they would've let me in if this had happened three months ago.

No one's ever seen you, Diary. No one knows about you. But I had to bring you. At the last minute I stuck you in my backpack. I didn't think I could go it alone.

And for all that Mom would notice, I could probably bring you out sitting right beside her. But I won't. That's why I'm in the bathroom now.

I'm almost as worried about Mom as I am about Dad. She's like a zombie, as though she's under anesthetic along with Daddy. Will she die, too, if he does?

They're so in love. So connected. They've been married forty years. And still smile when one or the other walks into a room. They still have eyes only for each other. I used be jealous that they always saw me as second.

I get it now. I feel the same with Chris. When I first see him, it's like the rest of the world fades away. I don't mean it to. It just does.

I don't understand why Mom and Dad didn't see that about me and Chris. Why didn't they understand? Why didn't they want me to have what they have?

Dad was in good spirits this morning, but he was a little groggy. They'd given him something before we got here. He joked with me about my problems in trig last semester. Said he hoped the doctors were more accurate when it came to measuring off the incision line.

He laughed. I didn't think it was funny at all.

And then Mom came in from talking to the doctor and they looked at each other for a long time. They were talking to each other. Saying really deep, serious stuff, except they didn't use any words.

A few minutes later, the orderlies came to get him. He glanced between my mom and me, and then, holding my gaze steadily, like he always did when he was about to teach me something, he said, "You're a good girl, Carol Bailey. The best. I love you."

I told myself I wouldn't, but I started to cry.

I'm not sure he saw, though. He was already looking back at my mother. I didn't hear what he said, but I saw them kiss. It was a long, gentle kiss. And made me cry harder. And then he was gone, and the room was empty.

It's been almost an hour now. I'm supposed to meet Chris in another ten minutes. I think I'll go early, just in case.

I can't wait any longer.

If I don't find some strength, I'm going to lose it and they'll have to haul me away before I find out how Dad's doing.

Please tell me he's still alive, Dear Diary. Please tell me that all is going as well as can be expected.

Please?

9:15 a.m.

I've got to go back to Mom. Chris held my hand for ten minutes. I feel much stronger.

He's sure Dad's going to be just fine. He reminded me that Dad's relatively young for this kind of surgery. And in good general health. He isn't overweight.

He warned me that it might be several hours yet, and that if it was, it didn't mean anything bad.

I don't know how right he is about any of it, but I need to believe him so I do.

He told me his mother said hello and that she's thinking about us. He's coming back at eleven.

11:10 a.m.

I only had a second with Chris. Mom's been crying and I don't want to leave her alone.

Still no word from anyone.

The day seems to have gone on for years already.

Chris insists that no news is good news. I have to accept that.

He's going to bring lunch from the deli around the corner when he comes back at one. I won't tell Mom who brought it.

I don't imagine either of us will be able to eat, but Chris says we must.

So I'll try.

CHAPTER NINE

1:25 p.m.

I finished the jigsaw puzzle. Saw Chris just long enough to grab lunch. I'm afraid to leave Mom except for these brief trips to the bathroom. I'm drinking so much diet soda I'm swimming in it.

She's having as much coffee.

We've been talking a lot. Like old times. But just about the past. Memories from when I was a little girl. I wanted to ask Mom about when she and Dad were dating, but I was afraid to bring up the subject. Afraid it would remind her of Chris and change her back into the stranger she's become these past days.

Neither of us touched lunch. But Chris is a smart man. He brought cold sandwiches and fruit. They'll keep.

In case you haven't figured it out already, Diary, there's still no word. That's almost six hours. I read the paper and found a seek-and-find but can't concentrate on it. Mom's doing a crossword puzzle. Or pretending to.

Chris tells me not to worry. It's hard to do. He hugged me, though, and it helped so much. For a second there, my stomach wasn't in knots.

I told him he didn't have to come back at three. I hate that he's making so many trips, walking down here, when I'm only seeing him for a few seconds.

He says the exercise is good for him. That he often takes walks during the day. And then he said something else that's been ringing in my head ever since.

"Your heart is hurting. I belong here with you, Carol. It's as simple as that."

And I knew he was right.

4:00 p.m.

Still nothing. It's been too long now. Something has happened that they didn't expect.

Didn't even talk to Chris at three. Just looked out the door of the waiting room and shook my head.

Mom's shredding the tissues I'm handing her. But she stopped crying hours ago.

My body is on fire and my face feels cold. I want to be out of this place. Out of this time.

And I want Chris.

He can't make my father better. But his presence continues to give me strength.

6:05 p.m.

My last time in this bathroom. Thank God for that. Dad's still alive!

I don't know any more, but I'm grateful for that much.

He came through surgery. And recovery. He's made it through the most critical part—for today. The future remains to be seen.

Mom's staying with him tonight.

She didn't like leaving me alone, but I reminded her that I'm an adult. And, truthfully, I welcome some time away from my parents. Life has become so complicated. So rife with potential pain that the fear engulfs me, even now.

My father's alive today, but these hours have shown me clearly that I have a tough road ahead of me, loving my parents as much as I do. They're only going to get older, weaker, from here on in. I have to be prepared for that.

I've never felt as alone as I do right now, Dearest Diary.

I had a few seconds with Chris at five. They'd just moved Dad into ICU. Mom was with him, and I was waiting my turn. We have to go in individually right now. And only for a few minutes. He's awake but barely.

He looked terrible, Diary. Worse than the ninety-year-old guy who sits in front of us at church. His lips were chapped and his eyes sunken and unfocused. He's trussed up with so many wires I don't know how they keep them all straight. And he has at least two IVs and various other tubes. He's on oxygen. Truthfully, I don't know how they can tell anything about the state of his body. I doubt it's doing anything on its own.

Anyway, I can't think about all of that now. I'm staying with Mom until nine and then driving home. Chris insists that he's going to follow me home. He doesn't like that I'm driving all that way by myself.

I told him it wasn't necessary, and I meant it. But I know he'll be here.

And I know I'm glad.

I need him.

11:45 p.m.

Chris just left. I'm no longer a virgin.

CHAPTER TEN

February 13, 2008, 8:05 p.m.

MONICA TURNED THE PAGE. And then another. Frantic now, she flipped through the rest of the pages in the leather-bound book. Blank. All blank.

How could that be?

Almost two hours had passed and darkness had fallen, outside and in her condo. Only the lamp by the couch was on, leaving her in an isolated pool of light as she sat there, feeling as though she'd finally met her mother.

All her life she'd heard about the woman who'd given birth to her. First from her father, who'd known her far too briefly and loved her more deeply than most people ever love. And then from Carol's parents, the grandparents Monica had sought out after his death.

Tonight, more than any other time in her life, she needed her mother. She should cancel tomorrow's appointment. Logically she knew that. But she couldn't bring herself to do so.

She wanted so badly to call Shane, to use the appointment as an excuse. Yet she was afraid that made her little more than a pathetic ex who couldn't let go.

If only Carol were there, if only Monica could talk to the woman who'd known more about life at eighteen than Monica knew at thirty.

Monica got up, retrieved her cell phone from her purse. Hit speed dial.

"Aunt Margaret?"

"Yes, dear, how are you?"

"I just got your package."

"Oh."

"Did you read it?"

"Some of it. But I stopped. I didn't think it was my business."

"It's my mom's diary."

"I know, honey."

"How long have you known about it?"

"A week. I mailed it to you the day I found it. It was up in the attic, in a box of my mom's linens, of all things."

"It talks about your mom. About Daddy caring for her." Monica had heard the story many times. "And it says that you were away at school."

"Finishing up that exchange program."

"Daddy was really hoping you'd make it back in time." Monica had often heard her father say that, yet tonight, after reading about it in her mother's girlish scrawl, the tragedy of those days seemed so much more potent.

"We all were, but I wasn't even close. Mom died on the 19th of February, 1977."

Only five days after Carol had slept with Chris.

"Do you know what happened between my mom and dad during those last days?" Did their relationship continue? "The diary ends on Valentine's Day. Did he ever see her again?"

"Once or twice. Mom took a turn for the worse on the fifteenth. Fell into a coma. It's my understanding that he never left her bedside after that. They'd told him it was a matter of hours. Those hours stretched into four days."

"How long did he stay in Chicago? To tie up loose ends?" These were questions that had never occurred to her before.

Suddenly, every second of those days mattered.

"There really weren't a lot of things to do," Margaret said in her soft, well-spoken, southern-lady voice. "He'd sublet an apartment, fully furnished, on a week-to-week basis. A family friend was forwarding his mail. As soon as the coroner released Mom's body, he flew her home to Tennessee. And never heard from your mom again, as far as I know."

Monica rubbed her brow. She needed aspirin. Another headache was beginning.

So many questions. "We know Mom was killed when she was driving to Tennessee. Surely she told him that much at least—that she was on her way to see him."

What Carol hadn't done was tell her father about her, Monica. And although Monica had asked both her father and her grandparents, no one had been able to tell her why.

"No," Margaret said. "He had no idea she was coming down."

"But he would've been thrilled! He'd have married her."

"I'm sure he would have, honey." Margaret's voice was wistful. "Your father was a changed man when he returned from Chicago. He resumed coaching the boys' track team that spring, taught summer school and then went back to teaching full-time in the fall. But he wasn't the happy-go-lucky guy who'd left Tennessee the previous year."

Her father had been the most revered, respected and intimidating English teacher in her high school. He'd had offers to move up in the educational system. Principalships, even an assistant superintendency, were offered to him. He'd always refused.

He'd been on the track, running by himself, when he'd had the heart attack that ultimately killed him at fifty-two.

"He never forgave my grandparents for my mother's death," Monica said, repeating something they both knew. "He was sure she didn't see that gravel truck she pulled in front of because she was so emotionally distraught at having to choose between them and him."

"Witnesses who passed her said she was crying while she drove."

"I know." Monica took a deep breath. "And he wouldn't let me have anything to do with them because of that. Yet, other than on that one issue, he never said anything negative about them." She thought of the pages she'd just read. The threats her grandparents had made. "And he could have."

"He took you from them," Margaret reminded her. "You were all that mattered to him at that point."

After the accident, the state police had called William and Martha Bailey as their unmarried daughter's next of kin. They'd turned over the baby who'd survived the accident to them.

"They didn't fight him."

"Your mother put his name on your birth certificate."

Even when they were living states apart, even though they weren't in touch, she'd reached out to her Chris. Acknowledged him.

That was the kind of love they'd shared.

The kind Monica had—used to have—with Shane.

All consuming. Incredible. Magic.

And short-lived?

CHAPTER ELEVEN

MONICA MADE IT AS FAR as her bedroom, taking off her pumps and tailored wool jacket, before the sight of the oversize queen mattress, the down comforter, reminded her of the man she'd expected to share that bed with for the rest of her life.

The man she'd intended to make love with in her eighties.

Darkness descended again. Not a darkness that could be dispelled by the flick of an electrical switch. She knew. She'd tried often enough. And with the darkness came the weight of a broken heart. Broken dreams.

The pain.

She couldn't do it. Couldn't go in there tomorrow and have herself injected with her soon-to-be-ex-husband's sperm. She couldn't bring on the heartache.

Like her father, she'd loved and lost.

She couldn't have Shane's baby without him. It wasn't right. Wasn't moral or decent.

Even if some small part of her hoped the child would bring them back together...

Had he been able to have sex with that beautiful stranger? Had he recovered from whatever had prevented him from making full and complete love with Monica?

The idea twisted her inside out.

Lying on the bed, staring at the ceiling, Monica tried to clear her mind, to focus on business, on the multimillion-dollar tooling company that would be going public in the morning, listing the clients she'd pegged for the buy.

She was okay again. Confident. Where she was most comfortable. As her father had taught her to be.

Her father. Chris. The man who'd walked to a hospital several times on that one day just to get a shake of the head. Who'd gone there simply because a girl's heart was breaking. The man to whom love was so important he'd been willing to risk everything—especially the career he'd loved—for the woman who'd captured his heart.

The man who'd given up months of his life to care, almost single-handedly, for the mother who'd spent her life caring for him.

Carol Bailey must've been some kind of woman. So young, yet so sure. Monica wasn't sure about much of anything.

So what happened? *Was* she conceived that Valentine's night? Counting the months to her November birthday, it seemed feasible. Of course Carol had been young. Monica could've been early.

And then, after Monica came, had Carol changed her mind? Had she suddenly decided she didn't really love Chris, after all?

Or did her father tire of the young girl once he'd had her in bed?

So much heartache. So many lives unfinished.

SO WHAT HAPPENED? Was Carol's determination just a result of her youthful enthusiasm? Was her absolute certainty in her love for Chris misguided? Had she been nothing more than a very young and idealistic kid whose courage was merely a disguise for ignorance?

Or had her mother died knowing she loved Chris Warren more than life? Had she gone to her grave faithful to that love?

Monica had to know. Period.

Throwing off her blouse, she strode over to the closet, stepped out of her panty hose and into a pair of jeans. Pulled on an off-white angora sweater that would keep her warm, no matter what the cold Chicago night brought her. With matching socks and a pair of brown lace-up ankle boots on her feet, she left the bedroom behind in search of answers.

She knew two people who had them. And this time she wasn't accepting any vague excuses or deferrals.

This time she had ammunition. A bribe if that was what it took.

Grabbing up the small leather book that explained so much and yet not enough, Monica headed out into the cold Chicago night.

CHAPTER TWELVE

GRANDPA BILLY WASN'T HOME yet from the wood shop at the assisted living facility where he and Grandma had moved ten years ago. Grandma was thrilled, as always, to have Monica come for a visit.

The apartment door was decorated with a wreath of rattan and pastel silk flowers.

Silk. Fragile. Just like her eighty-eight-year-old grandmother. Were answers really worth putting the woman she'd grown to adore through more pain? Hadn't Billy and Martha suffered enough? They'd lost their beloved only child before her twentieth birthday.

And lost the first twenty-five years of their only grandchild's life, as well.

Before she could decide, the front door flew open. And a small woman, an inch or so shorter than Monica's five foot four, stood there, framed by the light.

"Monica?"

Martha's voice wavered with age.

Monica nodded as she approached the shaky arms

reaching out to her and walked right into them. As she'd done the first time she met this woman. And every time since.

Which didn't explain the sobs that came from some-place deep inside her as she held on.

She *couldn't* explain. Couldn't think. She could only cling. And feel. And know that every time she saw this woman she'd come home.

MONICA HAD SO MANY questions. As she'd driven over to her grandparents', her mind had been filled with them. In the end, as she moved beside the old woman to a room filled with antique furniture that had been new to Martha Bailey at some point, she didn't have to ask. One look at the diary in Monica's hand and words poured out of her grandmother, as though the woman had always known this day would come. As though she'd been waiting.

As though she needed to speak the painful words as badly as Monica needed to hear them.

In the end, Monica just sat and listened.

"I met Billy Bailey when I was eleven. He was fifteen. His family had moved in down the block and he'd walk to school behind us. Every day. Always behind us, scuffing his feet, kicking stones. He never joined us.

"Never talked to us at school, either. The older kids on the block made fun of him. Made up outrageous stories about him and his family—probably just to scare us. They said he was an escaped prisoner holding his family hostage. And then one day, after he'd read a poem he'd written in English class, they decided he was some famous writer who was hiding out in our little neighborhood to avoid discovery.

"It turned out, of course, that he was just shy and needed an invitation to join us…."

"Which you offered him," Monica interjected and then, watching the faraway look in Martha's eyes start to fade, knew she wasn't going to do that again, wasn't going to bring her grandmother back to the present until she was ready. Martha was living another time, and she'd taken Monica with her.

It was a place she desperately wanted to go.

"I offered." Martha nodded slowly and paused. Monica waited patiently.

"We went on our first date when I was fifteen and were married on my eighteenth birthday. Oh…that was a day. So many flowers. And the music! I can still hear the waltz we danced to. At first just Billy and I were whisking around on that makeshift dance floor in my parents' backyard. Lights shone from the trees and people were gathered all around, forming a circle to hold us in. The circle of love, they called it. It was meant to keep us together forever…."

The young girl had danced, her heart filled with love and hope. She'd been secretly in love with Billy Bailey for seven long years and finally, finally he was hers.

She was a little nervous about the night to come. Wedding nights weren't pre-empted in those days, and while her mother had told her some things, it had only been enough to leave Martha with more questions, not to comfort or calm her. But when she danced in Billy's arms, when she felt his body pressed against hers and looked up to see those eyes, those lips, smiling down at her, she knew everything would be fine.

As it turned out, it was better than fine. Much, much better. And they began a glorious life. Billy worked at the *Chicago Tribune,* running a press, and rushed home to her every night when the other guys went out for beer. He read to her. Danced with her. Helped with the dishes and took her for long walks. She'd play the piano and he'd sit on the bench beside her and they'd sing. They'd play cards, either just the two of them or with friends. They saw their families often.

Some of these stories Monica had heard often over the past five years. Some of them she was hearing for the first time.

After her marriage to Billy, the years passed so quickly, Martha hardly noticed them. Until suddenly she did. She wasn't sure how it happened, but one morning she woke up and she wasn't eighteen anymore. She wasn't Billy's young lover. She'd had her thirtieth birthday. And she still wasn't pregnant. Her home was beautiful. While her friends had been making babies and formula and changing diapers, she'd made drapes and bedspreads and stained the tables her husband had built. She'd hooked rugs and crocheted doilies and bought pretty dishes. She'd grown flowers, planting gardens all over the yard, and harvested vegetables, too. She'd raised chickens, selling the eggs for money she saved to buy a brand-new living room set.

She'd just never had a baby grow....

But she had Billy. And on the days depression over-whelmed her, when her arms were too empty, her hours meaningless, he'd come home to her. He'd hold her. Take her for a walk. He'd tell her how she filled his heart, his life, how he couldn't live without her. How she'd made him the happiest man on earth.

And for a while, until the emptiness started to gape again, she'd believe him. She went to the doctor, but there was nothing anyone could do. No explanation or remedy for what ailed her. She talked to Billy about adopting a child. He agreed and for the next couple of years they looked for a baby to come their way, waited on a list that seemed never-ending. She'd built a nursery piece by piece. Sewed and painted and knitted little booties. And they never got the call.

She turned thirty-five and then forty. And spent six months after that crying every single day until Billy told her she had to shape up.

"A baby isn't meant to be, Marty. Not for us." Standing there in their bedroom, holding her upright after he'd come home from work and found her lying on the unmade bed, still in her nightgown with her hair a mess, he spoke more firmly than she'd ever heard.

Staring up at him, she felt the familiar tears against the back of her eyes, flooding her vision until he was little more than blur.

"I don't have to lose you, too," he said, more softly, reaching down to gently kiss her lips. "Now, come on. It's Valentine's Day and I'm taking you out. We're going dancing. You have half an hour to get yourself prettied up."

She didn't feel like dancing. Hadn't even known that the holiday for lovers was upon them. She went on crying.

"I don't have a present for you," she sobbed.

In years past, he'd have come home to his favorite dessert, a cherry cobbler that she doctored with her own secret ingredients. There would've been a nice dinner, too, but he would've gone for the dessert first. And then her. They might or might not have gotten to the dinner sometime later that night.

"You *are* my present, love," Billy said, and with the way he was looking at her, she could only believe him. "You've always been enough for me. Don't you understand that?"

Something happened to Martha then. Some constricting, suffocating emotion let go inside her. She stared up at the man she still loved more than her own life and felt a rekindling of the magic they'd always shared.

"I love you, Billy Bailey."

"And I love you, Martha Bailey."

"Show me?" she whispered, forgetting for the moment how she looked, still in last night's bed clothes, not even running her fingers through her hair.

"Yes," Billy said, not seeming to notice that he had a hag standing before him.

And over the next several hours, he made Martha forget that, as well. She was eighteen again, reliving their first time. And then the time they'd been on vacation in the wilds of Michigan. He took her to their tenth anniversary and the luxury hotel room he'd surprised her with, reminding her of the things they'd discovered about themselves there. In one night, he made twenty-two years of love to her.

And in the morning, Martha was eager to get up again. To start the day. And the new rest of her life. With a new goal. To spend every single minute being thankful for the man she adored, thankful that he adored her back. That very day, while Billy was at work, she walked down to the church and volunteered to help in whatever way she could. Three months later, she was providing regular meals to shut-ins. To the elderly who could no longer get around. And to young mothers with brand-new babies. To a friend of hers who had the flu, and a woman ten years younger who was dying.

And every night, when Billy came in from work, she was fully coiffed, with dinner on the table, a smile on her face—and more importantly, a smile in her heart.

And then came the day she got sick in the garden.

CHAPTER THIRTEEN

"YOUR MOTHER WAS AN angel sent from heaven to bless us," Martha told Monica, smiling at Billy, who'd returned and was drinking hot chocolate with them.

When she'd heard that Monica hadn't eaten dinner, Martha insisted on making her a grilled cheese sandwich and a mixed greens salad, which Monica ate sitting at the scarred wooden table in the kitchen while her grandmother fussed around, cleaning up.

Now the three of them sat at the old table, just as her mother had sat there with her parents years before.

Martha and Billy took turns telling stories about her mother's childhood. Stories she never tired of hearing.

Monica watched the memories play across her grandparents' faces. And then, so softly she was almost whispering, she asked, "So what happened?"

"There's something I didn't tell you." Martha's tone had changed. The nostalgia, the gentleness, was gone. She exchanged a long glance with Billy, and only when he nodded did she continue.

"During those years when I was busy growing flowers and prettying up my house, while my friends were all busy with the important business of raising human beings…"

Monica waited.

"I lost my head for a little while."

"After your fortieth birthday. I know. You told me."

Martha shook her head, the wrinkles in her neck more pronounced, in spite of the high-collared blouse she was wearing with a pair of dark slacks.

"Long before that. I can make no excuses, have no explanation. Other than that I married young—not young for the times, but young for me—and I'd never even looked at another boy from when I was eleven years old."

With no idea what was coming, Monica leaned forward, elbows on her knees, facing her grandmother. Martha took Billy's hand, met his gaze for another long moment. He smiled at her and it seemed that was what she'd been waiting for.

"I met someone," Martha said quickly. "A salesman. He came to the door one afternoon, selling shoes. I let him in and as he tried pair after pair on my feet, touching my calves, I just…lost my head. He made me feel desirable. Complete. Whole.

"To be fair to Billy, he did, too." Martha stared straight ahead. "It's just that Lance didn't know I couldn't get pregnant, couldn't give my husband the family we'd always wanted. He didn't know I felt like a failure."

Monica didn't want to hear any more.

"It's okay," she interrupted, placing her hand over her grandparents'. She didn't need to know this.

Billy coughed and then said slowly, "People get confused sometimes. It's part of being human."

Grandpa Billy didn't say all that much anymore, as though he was conserving his breath, but every time he did, Monica hung on his words.

"I hurt your grandfather more than anything in this lifetime ever hurt him," Martha said, her voice surprisingly strong.

Martha Bailey had strengths that her daughter had probably never known about.

"It only happened once," she said. "In my early thirties." She paused. "But it took me a lifetime to forgive myself for it."

The way she said those words told Monica something entirely different. Martha still had not, and probably never would, forgive herself for being disloyal to the man she loved. And even so, at forty, she was blessed with a miracle.

"Anyway," Martha continued, "the baby was born after an easy labor. Everything was perfect with Carol until just before her eighteenth birthday. We knew something had happened, we just didn't know for several months that it wasn't a *what,* it was a *who.* Overnight she changed on us. Grew distracted, didn't come home and immediately pour out everything about her day. She had a funny smile on her face, a bounce in her step. A confidence we'd never seen before. I told Billy she was growing up. And he agreed with me, although I think he knew...."

"In her Diary Mom wrote about your reaction when she told you about my father...."

With pinched lips Martha nodded. Before she could speak, Monica put two and two together.

"You were terrified that she was going to make the same mistake you did. Getting married to the first man she loved without looking around first to make sure that love was forever."

"If you don't know the bad, you don't know how great the good is," Martha said. "She'd never even gone on a date, not with him or anyone else, and suddenly she was absolutely certain she'd met the man she was meant to love forever. I'd learned what happened when the bad times came, when life didn't unfold like you'd thought it would and you started to doubt everything. Without any experience, how can you be sure about anything?"

Monica nodded, understanding her grandmother in a way she might not have six months before.

"For the first time in her life, she didn't put her father and me first. Our word, which had been gold until then, meant nothing anymore. I didn't know what this man had done to her, but he'd somehow convinced our daughter to trust him more than she trusted us, her own parents...."

So much pain. So much love. Monica, whose life had both, teared up again.

Shane had been her first love, too, so she'd had no

basis of comparison. Still didn't in that area. And she'd taken their love for granted—almost as though it was their due. She hadn't paid attention to her husband's struggles as she should have. Hadn't realized how deeply Shane's impotence had affected him over the past year. She hadn't truly realized the value of their love or her responsibility to watch over it.

"Grandpa…" Again she paused, the familial term falling so awkwardly from her tongue. "His surgery. Obviously it worked." She smiled at him.

And Martha took up where the diary left off.

After that fateful Valentine's night, Carol and Chris were never alone again for more than a minute. She'd spent the next few days at the hospital with her father, and his mother had worsened overnight. By the time Chris's mother died, Billy had been moved from ICU. He was expected to recover, but would require months of rehabilitative care at home. Carol and Martha were instructed to keep Billy's life completely stress-free— or at least as far as they could manage.

And Carol told Chris that she couldn't see him or speak to him until her father was better.

She promised to come to him, to find him in Tennessee, just as soon as her father recovered. She promised it would be no more than six months.

"She told me this on the day we had our last fight. She blamed herself for her father's heart attack— although it had far more to do with corroded arteries than with Carol's love life. She told me she'd given Chris her diary," Martha said, glancing at the book

Monica had carried to the table with her. "It was her promise to him. She was giving him her heart and she'd have to come and collect it.

"Of course, she didn't expect to find herself pregnant after only having slept with him on that one night. Nor had she counted on her father's reaction to the pregnancy.

"I'm ashamed to say," Martha said as she once again looked at her husband. "But Billy and I used his illness to keep her with us."

"We did, and we paid dearly." Billy's voice cracked.

Martha took over immediately. "Once we knew about the baby, we were more frightened than ever that our girl was going to tie herself to what we saw as a lecherous older man, a teacher who had an eye for young girls. We thought she'd feel obligated to promise herself to him for the rest of her life—without ever having the chance to find out what life held for her. We made a deal with her that she'd have the baby and we'd take care of it while she got her college education. If, after that, she wanted to marry Chris, we'd support that decision."

"But he wouldn't wait?" Monica asked.

"She had no intention of asking him to wait," Martha told Monica. "We just didn't know that at the time."

"To appease her father, Carol agreed to his stipulations. Looking back on it, as Billy and I did almost every day for the next twenty-seven years, we think she was just so darned relieved that the news of her pregnancy hadn't killed him that she would've agreed to anything."

Martha's eyes filled with tears. "And at first, when

Carol brought you home, we thought everything was going to be fine. We made it through Thanksgiving and then Christmas and she seemed to be settling in. She'd enrolled in the spring semester at the University of Illinois. You'd taken to breast-feeding like a natural and she seemed happy, content, as she cared for you, played with you. She took you everywhere."

Her chest tight, Monica waited as Martha once again paused. All the things Martha had told her that night had not seemed as hard for her grandmother as whatever was to come.

"Then, one day, she said she was going to Tennessee. Billy had just come from the doctor. He'd been given a clean bill of health.

"I panicked. I reminded her of the deal she'd made. I told her that if she left, she was not ever to step back in our house again."

Martha was crying in earnest now.

"She didn't mean a word of it," Billy said shakily.

"I regretted the words the second I spoke them," Martha said.

"You were desperate," Monica guessed. "Trying to scare her into staying."

"I killed her." Martha's tears had stopped, her eyes tired and old-looking. "She thought I meant what I'd said, and although she still left, she was crying while she drove…."

"You couldn't have known…"

"Thank God you were thrown from the car," Martha said as though she hadn't heard her.

"Grandma," Monica said, filled with sudden urgency. "Was Grandpa's heart attack my mom's fault?"

"Of course not!"

"But he'd just had word from his doctor about his heart problem, and she kept pushing you about Chris anyway. Hurting you. Causing you stress."

"She had no way of knowing…" Martha's words faded, her eyes widening. "I had no way of knowing…" she half whispered.

"I'd say our little girl here is maybe even smarter than her mama was, wouldn't you?" Billy said softly, his eyes on his wife. And then he looked at Monica. "I've been telling her for thirty years that it wasn't her fault."

Martha's shoulders relaxed in a way Monica had never before seen, and the tears in her eyes this time weren't quite as sad.

CHAPTER FOURTEEN

MONICA GAVE HER grandmother the diary. She sat between her grandparents on the living room couch as the old woman read aloud how very much her daughter had loved them, read about the grief Carol had suffered at the withdrawal of her parents. And read about the passion for Chris that suffused those pages.

"He came to get you after the state notified him of your existence when they discovered, upon your mother's death, that he was the father of the supposed orphan child. We told him then that we weren't going to interfere this time. That we'd wait for you or him to contact us before we saw you again."

"I didn't know that until he died and his lawyer sent me the letter telling me about you," Monica said, looking back, understanding now that her father had been a great man who'd loved hard and been deeply hurt but still preserved this relationship for her future.

Martha's sorrow, her regret, was obvious. That she and Billy had paid for their mistakes, which were really the desperate efforts of frightened parents to protect their only child, was very clear.

"We all make mistakes, my dear," Grandma replied when Monica said as much. "The key is to move on. Not to be afraid to try again. The key is to take that chance."

Chills spread through Monica's body and she knew she'd found, in the most bizarre, roundabout, unforeseen way, the answer she'd been seeking. She was going to call Shane.

Give him a chance to explain. Give herself a chance to forgive.

Tell him he didn't have to prove his masculinity in the arms of other women. That no matter what happened, he was all man to her.

And she was going to ask him to go with her to the appointment the next day. And if her luck was anything like her mother's and her grandmother's, who'd both conceived their babies on Valentine's Day, she, like them, would have a baby by Thanksgiving. A baby to love.

So would Martha.

Before she left, Monica told her so.

"SHE WAS NOTHING TO ME, Monica, I swear." Shane's voice came over the line later that night while Monica lay alone in the bed she should've been sharing with him. She'd asked him to come over.

He'd refused, preferring to stay in the two-bit motel room he'd rented back in December.

At least he hadn't moved into an apartment yet. Started buying his own furniture.

Or stripping parts of their condo.

"Did you… Were you able to—"

"I didn't even try," Shane broke in and Monica took her first easy breath in five days.

"Did you want to?"

His pause was answer enough and Monica's eyes filled with tears that dripped down the sides of her face.

"Of course I thought about it," he finally answered. "If my problems are because of stress, of trying too hard, or because of the pressure I put on myself to please you, then it stands to reason that being with someone else should work. And if it didn't, there'd be a bit of embarrassment, but nothing else to lose. It wouldn't matter."

Damn it, he made sense. He usually did.

"So why didn't you?" She lay in the darkness, not wanting to know, and asking anyway.

"Because I love you."

"Come home, Shane."

"I can't."

"Yes, you can."

"Not until I get this worked out. I was starting to resent you, Monica, to blame you, no matter how much I knew this situation isn't your fault."

Monica thought of her mother wrongly blaming herself for Grandpa Billy's illness. Of Grandma blaming herself for her daughter's death.

"That's only natural," she told the man she loved with all her heart. "And something we can work through together."

"I can't take that risk."

"Aren't you taking an even bigger risk that we'll lose each other by staying away?"

Shane didn't have anything to say to that.

Monica almost ended the conversation right there. Thinking about Shane's lips on another woman's, about a possible future liaison, she began to hang up the phone.

And a vision of Grandpa Billy staring into his wife's eyes, so obviously loving her, giving her the strength to tell their granddaughter about her indiscretion with that salesman, flashed before Monica's eyes.

That was the kind of love she wanted. The kind of lover she wanted to be.

"The insemination appointment's tomorrow."

"Are you going?"

Her grandparents had been holding hands when she'd left them a short time before. Ninety-two and eighty-eight, seventy years of marriage, and still holding hands.

"I want to."

"Okay."

"You don't mind?"

"No."

"Will you come with me?"

"No."

She wished Shane a good night and disconnected the call.

THE CONVERSATION played and replayed itself in Monica's mind as she lay on the paper-covered table in the small exam room at the clinic the next afternoon. They'd injected her half an hour before. She was giving those suckers a full hour to find an egg they liked and make a home within her womb.

She thought of her grandparents, whom she was going to see that night, to celebrate Valentine's Day. She thought of her father. And Carol Bailey.

She cried a little. And then some more. But by the time she was in her car, Monica's heart was more at peace than it had been in months.

As she pulled into her drive, her mind was on nursery furniture, pastel colors and asking Martha to teach her how to knit. Which was probably why she missed the tall, too-thin man sitting on the steps leading up to her front porch.

She didn't notice him as she stopped the car, got out and collected her purse.

"Monica?"

On her way to collect the mail from the box at the street, she froze. She'd imagined that voice there, in their yard, many times over the past weeks. It wasn't really surprising that it would visit her again.

"Monica." The voice was stronger, less questioning.

She turned, and just like that, he was there. "Shane?" She was afraid to hope, to read too much into his presence in their driveway.

It was the first time he'd been there since he'd left.

"You were right."

About what exactly? Monica was afraid to ask. Afraid…of everything.

Life without Shane was like that.

"I've been a fool, sweetheart, leaving you here all alone while I waited for life to take care of itself. My problems, your problems, whatever they might be, *are* life and that's what we promised each other."

Monica opened her mouth to speak—to agree with him, to ask if he meant what he was saying—but no sound came out.

And that was when her husband hauled her into his arms and covered her mouth with his own.

"Happy Valentine's," he said when he finally raised his head.

"Shane?"

Monica tried not to make too big a deal of it. Tried not to look down. But for the first time in months— since he'd walked out on her —she'd felt the rock-hard sensation that had occurred every single time Shane had held her in the old days.

"I know."

"You wanna try?"

"Every single day for the rest of our lives," he said, a new note in his voice. A peace she hadn't heard before.

Wanting to talk to him about that, to understand what he was thinking, to know everything about him, Monica's body urged her to other things first. Whether Shane could make love to her or not didn't matter as much as feeling her husband's skin against hers, running her fingers over him, *knowing* him.

Feeling his hands on her.

As though he could read her mind, Shane bent, lifted

her easily and carried her into the bedroom they'd shared for almost ten years.

Monica didn't want to rush, didn't want to push, didn't want to drive anything about their lovemaking. She just wanted to love Shane. It was all she could do. Her lips sought his, her hands moved over his body, and there was no thought of success or failure, of can or can't. They'd already succeeded. Shane was with her.

Together they could take care of everything else.

"I love you."

"I love you, too."

He was still hard.

And minutes later he began to move against her.

"You think it might last?"

"Looks like it." He was grinning. "Abstinence—and maybe the lack of tension—might be enough this time."

Monica's body welcomed the pressure of his while her heart sought something far more important. "Shane? I love feeling you inside me, you know that, but I love *you* far more."

"Me, too."

"I need to know that you love me more than you love this."

"I think I needed to know that, too," he told her. "I think that's what these last weeks were all about. When I saw that look in your eyes on Friday at the bar, I thought I'd lost you for sure. But then you called last night…"

"And?" Monica searched his face for reassurance.

"I came back," Shane said.

And in the end, love really was as simple as that.

EPILOGUE

November 13, 2008

Chicago Tribune:
Baby girl, born 4:03 a.m., 7 lbs, 13 ounces, to
parents Shane and Monica Slater.
* * * * *

Dear Reader,

I am honored to have been asked to be a part of this anthology celebrating the first anniversary of Harlequin's remarkable Everlasting Love stories. My admiration and respect for editors Paula Eykelhof and Beverley Sotolov is deep and heartfelt.

I have enjoyed writing a variety of romances over the past several years, but I am especially intrigued and excited by the concept of everlasting love, celebrating not the first rush of attraction turning into love as in traditional romances, but what it takes to nurture that love for a lifetime. I'm impressed by the quality of the stories I've read thus far, written by some of the best writers to come out of the romance genre. It was also a fun challenge to write this, my first-ever novella. As those who know me can testify, brevity is not my friend! It's easier for me to write 400 pages than to write only one paragraph, so writing "Our Day" was both a whole lot of fun and more than a little unnerving!

As always, I am deeply grateful for all the wonderful letters and e-mails I get from readers. Please feel free to contact me via my Web site www.jeanbrashear.com, or via postal mail at P.O. Box 3000 #79, Georgetown, Texas 78627.

Happy Valentine's Day to you and all those you love!

All my best,

Jean

OUR DAY
Jean Brashear

For Ercel, who makes every day Our Day

CHAPTER ONE

Austin, Texas

KITCHEN CLOSED until further notice, read the note propped on the counter beneath the telephone. The cook ran off to join the circus.

Jake Marshall squinted and read it again as he groped for a mug to fill with lifesaving coffee—

Which…wasn't there. The carafe was empty of all but sludge.

"Lilah?" The house had a different feel without her in it—too still, somehow. Sterile and cold, robbed of her unbounded energy.

He glanced out the window and saw Puddin' sniffing around. Though the dog was nominally his, Lilah was the one who babied the old guy. If she had really run away, she'd have Puddin' with her.

Jake grinned sleepily, shrugged and began assembling the makings for a fresh pot. She was pulling his leg, of course, but Lilah's mischief went down better after his brain was clicking.

The filters took a while to hunt down. When was the last time he'd had to make coffee? She was always up before him. He muttered a little before he finally located them. Now, was it one extra scoop for the pot or—

He gave up, shoulders drooping. He craved caffeine, tanker loads of it. Now. Last night had been a long one, with an emergency surgery lasting until nearly 2:00 a.m. *Okay, you can do this.* He dumped two extra scoops for good measure, then shuffled off to hit the shower while the coffee was brewing. On the way, he passed the dining room—

Oh, hell. Their anniversary. He'd missed it. No wonder Lilah had sounded funny when he'd phoned her to say not to wait up.

Man…everything still sat there—wilted salad, melting dessert. His favorite pot roast petrified in congealed grease. Lilah liked her house in order; she wasn't one to leave dishes soaking in the sink, much less food going bad on the table.

He was in deep doo, no question. This date was sacred, the anniversary not of their wedding but of the night they'd first made love. Our Day, they'd named it. For twenty-six years, the tradition had been special to them both. Even during the tumultuous child-raising years they'd never missed it.

He could plead the press of work, which was admittedly crushing since he'd switched to the trauma team. He was so tired half the time he could barely remember his name.

His colleagues thought he was crazy to leave a solid private practice, but he loved this work. Medicine interested him now in a way it hadn't in a long time.

Not more than Lilah, though.

Kitchen closed. Suddenly the note wasn't quite as funny. Lilah was such a gifted cook that friends had often urged her to open a restaurant or catering service. She might not be kidding, and for her to shut down her beloved kitchen...not good. He had some serious amends to make. Thank heavens it was nearly Valentine's. He'd have to go the distance to dig himself out of this hole.

As soon as he showered, he'd get busy cleaning up the dining room as a gesture of good faith. Lilah would be home soon, surely, and he'd apologize like crazy, then—

Upstairs, he heard his pager go off. And groaned. He was on call. Not a chance he could ignore it. He cast another glance at the mess, painfully aware that he barely had time to throw on clothes.

Not good. Really not good.

But Lilah loved him. He loved her.

It would all work out.

AT THE HEAD OF THE jogging trail, Lilah bent to tighten her shoelaces. Tried to focus on anything but Jake's absence and what that meant. Once they had been everything to each other; they'd had high hopes for their life together. So many dreams and plans.

One of those, recited like a mantra to each other

during the years of surviving the raising of teenagers, had been what life would be like when they were alone again.

Late mornings in bed. Long, lazy breakfasts, swapping sections of the paper. Time for travel, and most of all, to simply be with each other, relishing that while other relationships around them fell apart, they were more in love than ever.

Dreams now little more than vapor.

And Lilah was getting truly scared.

Missing Our Day was a shocking example, yes, but only one of many illustrating how far they'd drifted apart. Worse, Jake didn't seem to see what he was doing to himself. To them.

What he was risking.

She'd begged Jake not to work so hard, but she might as well have saved her voice. He didn't realize how often he slept on the couch in the den because he'd gotten in late and didn't want to disturb her. Or was simply so tired he couldn't manage one more step, much less muster the energy to undress.

It wasn't as though she couldn't entertain herself or didn't have her own interests—she had plenty of them. But throughout all the demands on both their time, there had always been a special corner of their lives they'd held inviolate. A space inhabited only by the two of them, a refuge where they shared hopes and disappointments, encouraged and healed each other, relived precious and very private memories. One of those was Our Day, their most sacred tradition.

If Jake could forget Our Day, they were in deeper trouble than she'd realized.

A date with her husband, an evening to reconnect, would have done wonders to settle her. To make the future seem less ominous.

It shouldn't be—they had so much going for them. Two of the kids were still in college—Zack already out, thank heavens—but their finances were solid, and the house was paid for. Gib would be out of school in May and Carla the next year, so it was nearly their turn to fly, hers and Jake's. They'd spent years looking forward to this time alone while they were still healthy and able.

But she'd married a latent adrenaline junkie, best she could tell. She stretched her quads, then slid into moves to do the same for her hamstrings.

Not that the signs hadn't been there, if only she'd recognized them. Diving off cliffs in Acapulco on their honeymoon. Bungee jumping for his thirtieth birthday.

He'd been a resident when they met; she'd been a bookstore clerk, one of a procession of forgettable jobs she'd held since she was fourteen. She'd always worked hard but never with a clear career path in mind. She'd continued to work until she'd gotten pregnant, helping to whittle away the mountain of student loans that had come along with Jake.

Of course she'd had to get used to being a medical widow at times, married to a surgeon on call. Surgeons were renowned jet jockeys with a stiff dose of God complex. Still, he'd been a devoted father and family man, who'd missed the important events of his children's lives only when absolutely necessary.

Who would have expected him to go bonkers at fifty-one and cross-train in trauma?

He was in excellent shape, but he wasn't young. Neither was she. If they were to fulfill those ambitions of travel and fun together, they'd have to do so soon, while they were still healthy and had the energy.

Instead Jake was obsessed.

And Lilah was struggling to keep her faith.

She straightened. Refused to concede to the tears behind her eyes. She held her head high and began to run.

CHAPTER TWO

"WHAT A NIGHT, huh, Doc?" asked Jake's favorite nurse, Stella, when they met at the coffeepot. "Lilah even get time to kiss you good-morning?"

He slugged down as much coffee as possible before responding, though it scorched his throat all the way. "She's okay." He studied the contents of his cup.

"Uh-oh. Look at me, Doc."

"What?"

"Don't go bein' all innocent on me. Man can't look me in the eye, he got somethin' to hide." She lifted an eyebrow. "How much trouble you in?"

"Not that much." He cut his gaze back to Stella. "I'll order flowers."

"Oh, boy. You missed somethin' important. Birthday? Anniversary?" At his wince, she arrowed in. "Son, you are a cliché, you know that? Aren't you ashamed, Dr. Golden Hands? Couldn't you at least screw up something original?"

Jake rolled his eyes. He hated that name, begun in his days as a renowned cosmetic surgeon. It was said that only God and Dr. Golden Hands could tell where your scars were and what procedure you'd had—no one else could begin to detect. He'd earned a tidy nest egg for Lilah and himself as his practice grew and grew.

Until he'd reached the day when one too many vain women, terrified of aging naturally, walked into his office, and he'd spent the entire consultation talking her into counseling, instead.

Yes, he'd had some opportunities to do meaningful work as a plastic surgeon; he'd performed pro bono procedures when possible, but he'd been determined to provide for his family as his own father had not. His mother had done her best, but her lack of education had meant a series of menial jobs. He'd wanted his children to have a full-time mom and was grateful Lilah had been of like mind.

At times, though, he'd felt that he'd sold his soul, catering to female insecurities, no matter how lucrative such a practice was, how much it meant he could do for his family. Finally he'd reached a point where he could not, in good conscience, continue.

"It wasn't our wedding anniversary," he protested. As if that helped. "And Lilah understands my work." Though he was less certain of that today. "She's a good woman. She'll be upset, but she'll forgive me. I'll make it up to her on Valentine's." Then an idea hit. "What time is it? Know a good cleaning service?"

Stella clucked her tongue. "Exactly how big a mess did you leave?"

"Pretty bad, I guess. But hey, things seem to be quieting down, so I'll just head home—"

They both heard the sirens. Jake sighed. On his way to triage, he paused at the nurses' station and spoke to the unit secretary. "Connie, if you'll do me this favor, I'll owe you my life."

Connie's face brightened. "Anything, Dr. Marshall."

"Order a dozen red roses sent to my wife—no, take that back, make it two—no, three." He scanned from one woman to the next. "Too much? What color says I'm sorry best?"

Nurses exchanged glances. Heads were shaking. "If you need three dozen to get you out of a jam," one said, "then all the roses in the world won't be enough."

"You don't understand my wife," he insisted. "She's a champ. She's sensitive to how important my work is."

"Uh-huh," said another. They walked off, chuckling.

The doors to the unit burst open, and one, then two gurneys raced inside. Jake felt the familiar surge of adrenaline ride roughshod over every other emotion. "Three dozen, Connie. With a note that says I'm sorry and I'll take care of everything." He was snapping on his gloves. "How about you? Got the name of a good cleaning service?"

"You made the mess," Stella said from behind him. "You'd best be the one to clean it up."

"Right—you're right. I left a note and told her I would. I just thought—"

"My advice, Doc? Don't think. Get ready to grovel."

"Lilah and I—we're solid. We'll be fine."

Then there was no time, only blood and pain and decisions to be made lightning-fast. So fast you felt more alive than at any other moment.

I'M SORRY. I was going to clean it up, but I got called in. Leave the mess for me. Love, Jake.

As she read the scrawled note on the kitchen counter amid spilled coffee grounds and abandoned filters, Lilah strolled, note in hand, to survey the dining room.

Contemplated, for the first time in their marriage, that she might have lost the man who had once been her reason for being. For breathing.

Oh, sure, there had been arguments, fights, disagreements. You couldn't live with someone for so long and not butt heads, to say nothing of how much the raising of children could strain the harmony between you. She had a temper, and he was pigheaded. They had different ideas about almost everything.

But somehow the marriage had worked. There had been spice in the friction. And love, so much love.

What concerned her now was that Jake seemed clueless about how his obsession with work was affecting them. Once family had clearly been at the center of his life, and his devotion had sustained her through the difficult parts of being a medical widow and a stay-at-home, jeans-clad mom whose handsome husband spent his days with beautiful women. Many of them fell at least a little in love with him, and had Lilah not felt so secure in his love, she could have been miserable.

But he'd always come home to her, always been faithful. Of that she was absolutely positive.

Which made dealing with this first-ever mistress so alarming. She could battle a flesh-and-blood woman; she had no idea how to win against the allure of high-stakes medicine. He'd cared about his patients when he'd been in plastics, but that concern paled against the siren call of trauma's life-or-death drama.

The kids were gone, and suddenly Lilah found herself almost an afterthought. She didn't believe he was doing it on purpose, but somehow his lack of awareness was even more painful.

She was excruciatingly aware that there was no telling how many years they had left together. When Jake's best friend, Bob Hunter, had died at fifty-two from a heart attack, the shock of it had made her resolve to stop putting off the adventures she and Jake had planned.

But the effect on Jake had been different. That was when he'd closed his practice and switched to trauma. Begun working even harder.

She was terrified of losing him, but when she brought up the subject, he reassured her that she'd be left a woman of means. He'd make sure she was taken care of.

Idiot. She didn't want money; she wanted him. Laughing together as they once had so often. Traveling the world or simply sitting on their deck in the moonlight, holding hands.

She'd brought up the subject on numerous occasions, though careful not to nag. He spent so much time at home in a haze of exhaustion that she was loath to disrupt what peace he could find here. She kept searching for the wake-up call that would get through to him. To let him know how much she missed him.

She could start that catering business friends urged her to consider, but while that would fill the hours alone, it would be only a half life, a diversion to deflect her from thoughts of what might have been.

They'd been so smug about the infallibility of their love—could she ever have imagined they'd be this out of touch with each other?

Jake Marshall, you big lug. She swiped at the tears she'd sworn not to shed. *Get a clue.*

She walked into the dining room with a trash bag to set the room straight. She thought better when her hands were busy, and the mess he wasn't here to see was driving her nuts.

The doorbell rang. She set the bag down and went to answer the door. The delivery guy was nearly invisible behind the explosion of roses.

Her heart melted a little as she accepted them. Well-tipped, the messenger left, and Lilah placed the bouquet on the foyer table. Opened the card. *I'm sorry. I promise I'll take care of everything. Love, Jake.*

"You'll mean to," she murmured. "Until you get paged again." With dragging feet, she returned to the dining room and cleared away the debris.

The roses were beautiful. Extravagant.

Impersonal. Money was not a big problem, thanks to the investments they'd made with the income from his former very lucrative practice.

Roses were too easy. She could accept them, forgive him whenever he finally arrived home, let things rock on this way, as they most certainly would if she let them.

But Lilah wanted Jake back. Her Jake. Yearned for him to look at her, really look, not have his vision clouded by exhaustion or worry over his patients, by the blinding light of being the key player in the struggle to preserve life.

What he was doing fell little short of a miracle at times, yes. He was proud of his work, and she was proud of him. She had no wish to rob his patients of his lifesaving skills.

But he wasn't the only physician on the planet, gifted as he was. He was taking too much of the load on his shoulders, and she was losing him, a slow bleeding out as deadly as any patient's.

There had to be some compromise, but thus far, she was the only one yielding. Jake Marshall had been her world for years, but sometimes lately she felt she barely knew him.

There had to be a road back for them. If she had to fight for him, then she would.

Even if it meant fighting dirty.

Inspiration hit. She raced through the cleanup and headed for her kitchen.

CHAPTER THREE

JAKE YANKED off his surgical mask, yawned really big and doubled over against the wall, stretching his aching back. Hours of surgery were hell on the skeleton; maybe he should check into that yoga class Lilah had urged him to take.

He stepped away and arched, then lifted his arms high over his head.

He could sleep for a week. Twelve hours in the sack sounded like heaven. Wrapped around Lilah, snuggled in their bed together—

Lilah. What time was it? He pulled his cell from his pocket and strode from the surgical wing to remove himself from all the telemetry. Down the hall that divided operating rooms from ICU, through the double doors that barred entry except during brief visiting hours, past the ICU waiting room—

A figure all but mowed him down. A tear-stained face greeted him. "Dr. Marshall? Are you Dr. Marshall?"

He barely had a chance to nod before the woman threw herself into his arms.

"Thank you—oh, thank you so much. My grand-daughter—you saved her. My son said—" She burst into noisy sobs.

The parade through the intersecting hallway that was the main artery of the hospital continued, an orderly grinning at Jake's discomposure, a nurse smiling, an EMT shaking his head as Jake awkwardly patted the woman's shoulder. "It's okay," he murmured. "It was—" *Nothing,* he'd started to say.

But that was wrong. The surgery wasn't as complex as many he'd done, but they had in fact saved the little girl's life. Not just him, the whole team. Once more, pride swelled in him. What he was doing made a difference. This—moments like this, here in the beating heart of a trauma center, where events were so often balanced on a tenuous edge, hope off one side, agonizing loss on the other—

There was nothing like being sure that what you did mattered. That you could, with luck and skill, restore a person to those they loved. Battle death and win.

His hollow stomach, his tired feet, the exhaustion he'd felt for hours…all of them vanished in this one shining moment, and Jake closed his phone, stuck it in the case attached to his waistband—

And settled in to let the older woman cry it out.

Feeling like a million bucks.

A FEW MINUTES LATER, after being introduced to the rest of the family and chatting with them about how long the little girl's recovery would require, Jake departed, eager to share with Lilah what had just happened.

Near the wall of glass where he could obtain decent reception, he dialed his home and waited.

And waited. When Lilah's voice-mail message started, he listened to her and smiled. At the beep, he began. "Babe, I wish you were here. I just worked on a five-year-old girl who was hit in a drive-by shooting." The injustice rolled over him again. "What the hell are people thinking?" He choked back his outrage and continued. "But she's going to make it. Her family—they treated me like I was a superhero. Her grandmother kept crying and hugging me and—" Then he remembered the purpose of his call. "I'm really sorry about Our Day, sweetheart. I'll make it up to you, I swear." He lowered his voice to a near growl, one he knew got to her on a visceral level. "I'd like to be doing some making up right now, if you catch my drift."

Someone brushed past, and he cleared his throat. "Um, Gruenwald got delayed, so I have to stick around awhile. The second I can, though, I'll be home. I'm going to grab a bite while the coast is clear, then—" Sirens sounded, and he groaned. "Damn. Gotta go. I love you, Lilah, so much."

He snapped his phone shut and charged down the hall.

Two and a half hours later, Jake's butt was seriously dragging as he approached the tiny break room off the E.R. administrator's office, but worn-out as he was, he couldn't help noticing the crowd spilling out the door. He frowned and tried to skirt past because all he wanted to do was be home and horizontal as soon as possible.

But someone hollered his name. "Yo, Doc. Your woman is amazing."

His head snapped to the side. "What?"

"Come here," said Stella. "Let him through, you hogs. Let the man have a chance at the goods."

A path widened for him, and he spotted what the fuss was all about.

A spread, the likes of which made his mouth water, filled the entire table. Fat clumps of grapes, plump strawberries, an array of meats and cheeses, vegetables, crackers and dips. A variety of pastries that smelled like heaven.

Vintage Lilah. Despite the fact that every hand he saw was full, there was plenty of food left, and all of it beautifully presented.

"You are one lucky son of a gun, Marshall," said a male nurse he was certain belonged to ICU and not the E.R.

Jake glanced around and saw that the crowd held many more people than simply trauma personnel. Lilah understood their lot; the staffs housed in this wing seldom got proper breaks to go eat. Everything they did was about speed and immediacy. The lives under their care couldn't wait for someone to return from a leisurely meal, and the people here were dedicated to an extreme degree. Long shifts, high pressure and little downtime exacted a toll.

Damn. What a woman. "I am," he responded, and ducked Stella's gaze. He'd screwed up so badly and what did Lilah do? She made him a feast. Sure, she'd cooked it for all of them, but he knew whom she was really caring for.

Him. Lucky son of a gun Jake Marshall.

Starving Jake Marshall. He dove in, snagged a handful of food and wheeled to go.

Home to Lilah.

"Wait—" The unit secretary grabbed his arm.

"Uh-uh. I'm way overdue to leave."

"I understand. But she sent you something special."

Jake spotted a bag in the woman's hands, with his name on it. He accepted it and resumed his departure.

"Hey, Doc, you're not going to let us peek?"

Recalling all the times Lilah had packed him a lunch and slipped in something private and often racy, Jake shook his head. "Nope." And winked before he left. To the sound of whistles and jeers and laughter.

Excellent stress relief. *Thank you, Lilah. From all of us*.

He practically inhaled the food as he loped toward the doctors' locker room. Once inside, he made certain he was alone before he opened the bag, already grinning in anticipation.

Then he frowned.

A package of underwear. With a note.

Here. Thought you might need this.

No signature. No *Love, Lilah*. No sketched heart.

Why would he need new underwear? There was plenty at home, always clean and folded in his drawer.

What had that note in the kitchen said?

The cook ran off to join the circus.

But she'd made food for them, when she'd said the kitchen was closed. Food meant love to Lilah; she'd always told him she put her heart in every meal.

She wouldn't actually leave him.

Would she?

Jake didn't wait to change; he remained in his scrubs, simply tossed his clothes and shoes in his gym bag and seconds later was out the door.

CHAPTER FOUR

"NO, I'M NOT CRAZY," Lilah said to her sister, Belinda, as her car barreled down the road.

"Don't bet on it. You have a man—a hunk, by the way—who's never so much as winked at another woman. Who loves you to distraction, has provided for his family and, despite a very busy career, missed few of the kids' plays and games and recitals—and you're leaving him?"

"You don't understand." Lilah couldn't blame her sister. Belinda's ex had not only cheated on her but was frequently behind on his child support. "Everything's different now."

Belinda's sigh was loud. Frustrated. "He still returns home to you, Lilah. He loves you. How bad can it be?"

Lilah chewed at her lip. Decided. "He forgot Our Day."

"Oh. Wow." Belinda had babysat their children many a year so that this one inviolable celebration could go on. "But maybe he—"

"Belinda," Lilah said. "Please be on my side right

now—" She couldn't keep the tears from her eyes. "I don't want to do this, Bee, but nothing gets better. He's like an addict who doesn't believe there's a problem even when his arms are covered with needle marks." She blinked hard. "I've talked to him, made excuses for him. That what he's doing is so important only makes things worse. But I'm scared to death of winding up like Bob Hunter's wife, Linda. I've got a lovely home and no financial worries, but I didn't marry a house or money. I married a man I hardly ever see anymore." She sniffed back sobs. "I miss him so much."

"Of course you do." Belinda became solicitous. "I'll put the coffee on. It'll be ready by the time you get here."

"Puddin's with me. Is that all right?"

"Okay, now I really am worried. You've kidnapped Jake's dog. That's serious stuff."

"He'd starve to death if I left him there." Lilah stroked the head of the gray-muzzled mutt. "And he's my dog, too." Though it was Jake who'd found him and brought him home. Ever the savior.

"The kids will be thrilled. Everybody adores Puddin'."

"Thanks, Bee." Lilah swiped at her cheeks. "I love you."

"Love you, too, big sis."

Being the sister in need was hard. Most often, Lilah had been the one who'd had things wired, who'd picked up the pieces when Belinda's luck had gone astray. It had been a point of pride for Lilah that she had the perfect family, the dream home, the complete package.

She wanted that dream back. She longed to turn around and go home. Let Jake have one more chance.

But she was very afraid that nothing would change if she did.

So Lilah petted the dog for comfort.

And kept driving.

HE JITTERED HIS KNEE at stoplights. Tapped the steering wheel. Drove like a maniac down the freeway, gripped by dread.

She wouldn't. She loved him. He loved her. They were two halves of one whole, had been for years. She'd never given him any reason to worry about her devotion—

I thought we could go to Fredericksburg this weekend. Check out the shops, stay in a B&B, the way we used to. Do a little Christmas shopping. Her eyes, so huge and green and beautiful. Hopeful.

I'm on call.

A frown marring her lovely face. *You were on call last weekend, and the one before.*

Davis needed someone to help him out. They have that new baby.

You're exhausted, Jake. You have to have a break.

I'm fine, babe. We'll go on my next free weekend, okay?

A quick swivel of her head, but not before her disappointment registered. *Sure.* She'd continued cleaning the kitchen. He'd left for the hospital.

That had been how long ago? He attempted to calculate back, but the days and weeks blurred together. He'd meant to make good on his promise, but one of the kids had decided to visit, then there'd been the holidays…

Images of guttered candles and dinner gone stone-cold.

The cook ran off to join the circus.

Here. Thought you might need this.

"She'll be there," he muttered. "I'll explain. I'll clean up. Take her out to dinner." Though he was having trouble putting one foot in front of the other.

At last, he wheeled into his drive and hit the garage-door-opener button, willing her car to be inside.

But only emptiness greeted him.

Damn it, Lilah. Okay, so you're angry. I don't blame you. She had a temper, but it flared and died just as fast. He'd busy himself clearing the mess, then catch a shower while he was waiting for her to arrive.

He walked into the kitchen, the silence deep and hollow. Barren. He thought about how seldom he'd entered their home—any home they'd occupied—without Lilah there, waiting for him. However harried she might be by the demands of family, the carpools, school plays, homework assignments, dinner parties, holidays—by some magic, she reigned at the center of their universe, a queen in blue jeans and sneakers who made it look easy. Who might blow her stack now and again, but who surrounded them with the knowledge that they were cherished. That comfort was to be had at any moment.

That they were safe, all of them, secure in her love.

Here he was in the heart of her domain, the kitchen,

and he felt her absence keenly. Home was just a building without her in it.

Dread curdled in his gut as he made his way to the dining room, predictably ordered and sparkling despite his promise to deal with the debris.

The roses—his roses—stood in the center, lush and gorgeous—

And wrong. So wrong. Stella had nailed it. Roses were a cliché, however profuse their number, and they were not Lilah at all. She was a unique mix of exotic and down-to-earth—she'd like bird of paradise mixed with geraniums. Daisies and bluebells. A fistful of wildflowers he'd picked himself.

Jake stood in the framed opening and pictured her face when the roses had arrived. Surrounded by the remains of a meant-to-be-special dinner she'd labored over.

Heard her voice in his head.

You're working too hard.

Could you take some time off?

We're not getting any younger, Jake.

The words had been a fly's pesky buzz he'd flicked away. What he was doing was crucial—didn't she get that?

I miss you.

More crucial than that?

He detoured to the backyard. He'd play with Puddin' for a while since he'd barely seen the dog in days. Then he'd shower and be ready when Lilah returned. He'd phone in sick and spend the next two days in bed with her.

He whistled for his dog. Clapped his hands and called out, "Puddin', come on, buddy. Let's throw the ball."

But the dog was gone, too.

Still he clung to hope as he raced up the stairs, yanked open the closet, pored through her dresser drawers, scanned the vanity in their bathroom.

Got hopping mad at first. *Lilah, why the hell didn't you hang around? Talk to me?*

I miss you.

She'd talked, all right.

He just hadn't been listening.

Jake sank to the bed, head in hands. He had to think, to figure out where she might be. He'd follow and plead his case. He'd make her understand that he was sorry.

Man, what a day. He sagged back. *Just for a minute,* he thought. *Only to clear my head.*

His eyes drifted shut.

Seconds later, he was out.

CHAPTER FIVE

"THAT TICKLES, Aunt Lilah!" Her nephew, Thad, wriggled in her lap as she buried her nose in his neck.

Was there ever a better smell than little-boy sweat? Slightly acrid, salty with an undertone of grass and leaves—

She squeezed him more tightly, just for a second, then growled, as he'd like much better. "Too bad, Sky Master. I have you in my power, and you're not getting loose." Her fingers tucked into his sides and began a dance designed to make him writhe.

"No—help! Save me, Mom!" Thad giggled, squirming like an eel to escape the tickling. "Aunt Lilah, no—" He nearly fell off her lap, but Lilah caught him in time.

Then lost her balance. "Oof—"

Thad escaped and shot to his feet, arms thrown high in the air. "I win! Score, Sky Master, one—" He cast her a mock-sneer. "Ancient Aunt Lilah, zip."

"Ancient, huh? I'll show you—" Lightning-quick, she leaped.

He skipped away, squealing his delight. "Can't catch me, can't catch me—"

Puddin' barked and circled them. Lilah charged after Thad, who squealed his delight. He whirled to head down the hall—

And ran smack into his mother, who was loaded down with linens for the sofa. Belinda grabbed him with her one free arm. "Have you finished your homework, young man?"

"Aw, Mom. Aunt Lilah and me—"

"And I—" Belinda corrected.

Thad rolled his eyes. "Aunt Lilah—" He cast Lilah a grin. "Young Aunt Lilah and I were just taking a break. Weren't we?"

Out of breath, Lilah lifted an eyebrow. "If you think I'm helping you out now, you are severely wrong, my man."

"Young, beautiful Aunt Lilah?" His mouth curved.

"You're out of luck, champ. The mom is here now. Better go do your homework."

"Man…You're no fun, Mom." But his eyes sparkled.

"And don't assume I'm not proud of that." Belinda brushed his hair from his forehead.

A pang of sheer envy hit Lilah, and not because few things disturbed Thad's sunny demeanor—after all, he wasn't a teenager yet. Plenty of time for that to change.

But even in the worst of the roller coaster of her kids' adolescence, she'd loved being a mother. Couldn't get enough of having her chicks around her, never mind that they'd brought platoons of friends and noise with them. She'd cooked enough for an army day after day and had felt honored that her children's friends preferred her house over their own. She'd dried tears and planned campaigns to win over crushes, counseled this one to forgive his dad and that one to deal with her mom.

Every day had flown by so swiftly that it wasn't until Gib and his friends had all gone off to college that she'd had a moment to catch her breath.

She liked the silence, the freedom. She *did*. Hadn't she prayed for this day?

Yet as she watched her nephew do his little-boy skip down the hall to his room, her heart twisted. "They grow up so fast, Bee."

"Is that the real issue?" Her sister clasped her hand. "You miss the kids?"

"No. I told you—"

The telephone rang, and Lilah didn't get to finish. As her sister headed to the kitchen, Lilah called out, "Remember—you promised."

Belinda picked up the phone. "Hello?" Then she glanced at her sister. "Hi, Jake." She listened, and Lilah could sense her waffling. Belinda adored Jake, and the feeling was mutual.

Lilah fired off her sternest glare.

Belinda's shoulders sank. "No, I haven't seen her. She's probably just run out for something, you think?" Her brows snapped together. "She took the dog, huh? Has anything happened between you?"

"Oh. Wow. Missing Our Day. That's pretty bad."

Belinda's voice went soft. "She loves you, Jake. Don't forget that. Of course I will." She frowned at

Lilah. "It would be stupid of her not to give you a chance to explain."

Lilah threw up her hands. Great. Just great.

"But maybe you two just need some time together. You've been putting in a lot of hours lately."

Okay, good girl. Thank you.

"Well, of course you're doing all this for her," Belinda soothed. "You've worked hard to take care of your family."

Lilah moved to stand square in Bee's path, hands on hips. She made a slicing motion at her own throat.

Bee's expression was both guilty and helpless. Lilah could hear Jake's voice on the other end, and for a second, she was tempted by the beloved sound of it.

She had to resist. Yes, she loved him. Missed him already.

But she'd done little except miss him for months now. If she caved this soon—

"Have you checked with the kids?" Bee asked.

Lilah was horrified. She grabbed her sister's arm. *Leave the kids out of this,* she mouthed.

"Absolutely. They'd only worry." Mutiny was on Belinda's face.

Lilah held her breath.

"Listen, Jake, Thad's asking for me. Can I call you back?"

Lilah's eyebrows rose to her hairline.

"That's okay. You get some sleep. I'm sure you're exhausted. Do you have anything to eat?"

She was going to kill her little sister. The man had plenty of money to order food.

And anyway, she'd left some things in the refrigerator, despite her threat.

"Oh." Bee's mouth quirked. "That was sweet of her. See? She does love you. Everything will be fine." At Lilah's disgusted expression, Belinda simply stuck out her tongue. "Yes, I promise. If she contacts me, you'll be the first to know." She said goodbye and hung up the phone.

"What are you doing? You said you wouldn't take his side. You can't make promises like that."

"If you'd go home, I wouldn't have to lie again." Belinda's face got that stubborn cast she'd perfected as a child. "I love him, too, Lilah. He's a wonderful man. I don't like being a part of hurting him."

"And I do? There's nothing I'd rather do than race home and fall into his arms—" She stopped. Exhaled. "This isn't fair to you. I'll check into a hotel."

"No, you won't. Besides, what about Puddin'?"

"I'll put him in the kennel."

"He's old. He should be in his yard."

Lilah fought not to burst into tears. "Of course he should. I want to be home, too, but I'm fighting for my marriage." She collapsed into a kitchen chair. "I'm making this up as I go, Bee."

She wished more than ever for her mother's guidance, her steady hand, but her parents were both gone now. "My husband, whom I love more than life, has never been further away from me. He's so thrilled with what he's doing and it's important, yes, but—" Then she voiced her deepest fear. "I'm scared he's going to wind up like Bob. That this new career will kill him."

Belinda bent to her, wrapped Lilah in her arms. "I am so sorry. I didn't understand." Their roles reversed, for a change, younger sister rocking the elder. "Don't you dare leave. I'll lie to him if I must because this is important. You two belong together. But, Lilah—" She drew back. Lifted her sister's head. "You will have to face him at some point and hash this out."

"I understand. But so far when I've tried, all he hears is nagging. Anyway, maybe he's tired of me. Perhaps the magic is over."

"You didn't hear his voice. The man is worried. He's not going to wait long before he calls in official help and your face winds up on TV. The only thing that's holding him back at the moment is his shame. He's aware that he screwed up. He just doesn't get the big picture yet."

"I can't stand the thought of getting anyone else involved."

"Except your poor sister, who hates deceiving the man she's had a crush on since she was fifteen?" Belinda grinned.

"You can't have him." Lilah sniffed and straightened. "Knothead though he is, I am not giving him up without a fight. He's going to have to tell me he doesn't want me anymore." Her heart clenched at the mere thought.

"He's a knothead, maybe, but he's not insane. You're the best thing that ever happened to him." Bee shook her head. "More's the pity. He is hot, you know."

"He is." Lilah's voice lowered. "But I can't say the same. My figure's going, and my hair's turning gray. I'm not the woman he married."

"Don't be an idiot. Jake's sexy for an older guy, but he's aged, too. Neither of you is anywhere near decrepit, though. Plus there's always the little blue pill."

"Not that it's any of your business, but when he does manage to be home and not dead on his feet, that's not an issue."

"Have you considered seducing him?"

"Please." She rolled her eyes. "Of course I have. This isn't solved with a great round of sex."

"No need to rub it in. You think you're deprived— I'm single with two kids. I'm not sure I remember how."

Instantly Lilah was reminded that her sister's lot was not an easy one. "I'm so sorry."

"Well—" Belinda's tone was tart "—you should be." Then she grinned. "Here's a suggestion. I'll put the kids to bed. You grab the wine. We'll have a pity party and trash the Y chromosome half of the species."

"It won't fix my problem, Bee."

"Mine, either. Let's do it anyway." Belinda winked, but Lilah spotted the loneliness beneath her sister's bravado.

So she nodded. "Why not?"

CHAPTER SIX

JAKE BOLTED AWAKE, drenched in sweat. Hard and aching from a dream of Lilah one summer night when the kids were off at camp, he extended a hand to draw her close—

And encountered air. Empty sheets.

She loves you, Jake.

Did she? How was this love, to just pull up roots and leave? He'd never expected anything like it from her.

He launched himself from the bed, in no mood to concede that most of her belongings were still in the house, that he'd broken a sacred tradition. She was gone, damn it, and she should be here. How the hell could they resolve anything if she'd vanished?

But the word itself sent a small shudder through him. *Vanished.*

Every day in his work, he witnessed how easily a loved one could be lost. One moment a person was riding in a car or walking down the street or simply sitting in a chair and—bam. Life, so rich and potent, snuffed out in an instant. Or bodies shattered in such a manner that they'd never be the same.

No. Not his Lilah. She couldn't be taken from him so effortlessly. He'd fight the devil himself for her—

He grabbed the phone, heedless of the hour. Dialed her cell. This was stupid. He'd missed an anniversary— okay, an important one. *The* important one. But they could talk. Work things out.

Assuming he could find her.

The phone kicked to voice mail. "Leave me a message," said the beautiful half-husky tone that even now had the power to reach down inside him.

"Lilah, where the hell are you? This isn't funny. I don't know what you're trying to prove—" *Great, just great. That'll bring her back.* One steadying breath, then, "Come home. I'm—" The beep signaled the end of the message right in the middle of "—worried."

He stared at the receiver in his hand. Stifled the urge to throw it out the window. Debated another attempt. Not that it would help. He had to see her. Be with her. Hold her and everything would work out.

Where was she?

Jake tossed the phone onto the mattress. By the second bounce, he was already starting the shower.

No more sleep tonight.

Might as well work.

LILAH JOLTED when the phone chirped with the salsa tune she'd chosen as her ring tone. She clasped it to her belly and skittered across Belinda's living room before the sound could awaken anyone else.

Once inside the kitchen, she glanced at the display.

Her home number. Jake.

She hesitated. She needed to have her act together when they spoke. That first contact was all-important, would set the tone for whatever happened next.

She wasn't ready.

She wished she hadn't left the phone on; doing so actually made little sense when she didn't dare speak to Jake, but she'd had some notion of remaining available to her children, however unlikely it was that they'd contact her. Zack did so infrequently. Carla and Gib were barely back from Christmas break and had both been more than ready to return to school and their friends.

Anyway, they'd try home, not her cell at this time of night.

Panic struck. What if he was phoning because something had happened to one of them? She clicked the On button. "Jake?"

The dial tone greeted her. She hit Off, then prepared to dial her house.

The voice-mail icon brightened her screen. With haste she selected it.

Lilah, where the hell are you? This isn't funny.

She sank back against the pantry wall. Blinked at the broom gone wavery behind the moisture stinging her eyes. He didn't sound sad or lonely or any of the emotions Belinda had attributed to him.

He was mad, pure and simple. Aggravated. Demanding.

She let her head fall against a shelf. Maybe there was

no hope for them. The first sound of his voice in nearly three days, and there was no love in it, not even luke-warm fondness.

Now she was really frightened. What if they were one of those couples who simply grew apart? Had nothing in common after the children left? He'd made a sharp left turn in his career and caught her by surprise—who was to say he wasn't itching for a change in his personal life, as well?

Profoundly unsettled, she huddled in her sister's pantry, pondering whether the marriage that had once been nearly perfect—crazy, chaotic, but perfect in its own way—was over.

Or had been a figment all along.

Her heart was as cold as the grave at the mere notion. She couldn't think what to do. If she'd been at home, she'd have flipped on all the lights and begun cooking or something.

But she was in her sister's apartment, and Belinda had to be at work in a few hours. The kids must go to school.

The click of claws outside the door sent a shudder through her. Puddin' whimpered.

Lilah opened the door, limp with relief. "Hey, boy." She drew him near, wrapped her arms around him as if he were the only thing solid in her world.

He released one of his old-dog groans and licked her hand.

Lilah let Jake's dog comfort her and wondered if Jake himself would ever do so again.

JAKE STORMED from the doctors' locker room and made his way to the E.R.

Stella was standing at the desk and frowned. "What on earth are you doing here?"

"Work." He surveyed the quiet room, then picked up a random chart and started reading.

One caramel hand slapped on top of the words. "I repeat—what do you think you're doing here? You've put in overtime and then some. Go home to your wife."

"I would if I had one," he snarled.

Stella's glance was razor keen. "Uh-oh." She snagged his arm. "Come with me."

He shook her off. "I'm busy."

"Uh-huh. I can see that." She nodded at the paperwork. "You're such a fan of reading closed charts on their way to be filed." She tugged again. "You following me or do I have to get rough?"

"Buzz off, Stel." He glowered at her.

But Stella hadn't reigned over the E.R. for twenty-one years for nothing. "If you got some notion you're scaring me, Doctor—" her tone was witheringly formal "—you are one crazy white man." She sighed. "Not that you aren't already managing a dead-on imitation of a fool."

Jake closed his eyes. Exhaled. "Look, I know you mean well—"

She grabbed him by the ear, and he yelped. Up to this point, they'd been whispering, however harshly, but now the entire staff had come to attention.

It wasn't every day you saw a five-foot-three woman tow a six-foot-four man by his ear as though he were in grade school and on the way to the principal's office.

"All right, blast it." Jake glared at her with the full force of his doctor-as-god authority. Pivoted on his heel and marched toward the hall between the E.R. and the surgical suites.

If he'd hoped to intimidate her, he was doomed to be disappointed. Stella strolled along, her chin in the air, her manner unrepentant.

He slouched against the wall like a surly teenager.

She halted in front of him, and he braced for the kind of lecture she gave so freely.

But she surprised him when her eyes went soft and worried. "Talk to me, Jake." She touched his forearm and squeezed. "Lilah?" Her voice was pure sympathy.

He found himself absurdly near tears and looked away until he'd mastered them. His shoulders sagged. "She's gone."

"What do you mean gone?"

"Packed up. Disappeared. Took my dog."

"Uh-oh."

"I don't know whether to be angry as hell or frantic. What if something—" He couldn't say it.

"She's okay."

His glance was swift. "You can't be sure."

"We're here and she's not. That's a good sign."

"But she could be—" He choked. Anywhere. Hurt. Lonely.

"Yes, she might be injured or in trouble, but it's probably her heart that's hurt, not her body."

"I screwed up, okay? It's a special date—the most special date, all right? But you don't just leave someone because they make a one-time mistake. Not when you love each other the way we do."

"Have you told her?"

"Of course I have. I tell her all the time." But then he tried to recall when he'd last said it to her in person. *Love, Jake* on a note acknowledging a mistake—did that count?

"Jake—" Another squeeze of his arm. "Have you studied the schedule lately? Noticed how often you're here instead of at home?"

"It's a busy E.R. I can't just—"

"Stay home?" she asked. "Of course you can. What, you imagine you're indispensable?" Another pat. "You're good, Jake, really good. We do need you around here, but we managed before you got here, and this place will rock along without any one of us after we're gone. It gets in your blood, trauma does, the rush of fighting back death, of caring for people at the worst moment of their lives. But you know the body can't live on adrenaline indefinitely. You wreck your health, and you're no good to anyone, not your patients and certainly not the loved ones who never see you anymore."

Jake swallowed hard. Was that him?

Hadn't Lilah been saying that, only not so bluntly?

And when had he last held her? Made love to her? Started a simple conversation, lolling in the porch swing or lying in bed, talking about their dreams?

"So what now, Stel? If that's true, how do I fix it?"

Stella chuckled. "You been living with a woman how many years and you don't have some notion of how to sweeten her up?" Her smile faded. "This might be beyond a quick fix, but my advice would be to track her down and do something unexpected. Something romantic. You remember how, or you want lessons?"

He wasn't sure. Romance, once such a part of them, had been in short supply for a while now. How long?

Have you studied the schedule lately?

He hadn't. All he could handle was making it from day to day, struggling to stay strong, to keep his focus sharp.

He was tired. Exhausted, really. Everyone on the E.R. staff was younger, many by fifteen or twenty years.

"Let a friend give you some advice?" Stella asked.

Wearily he nodded.

"I got no problems calling in favors to cover you for at least a week. Let me do this for you. For Lilah, who is a woman I respect." She paused. "Not the least for her ability to live with a surgeon for so many years and not murder him in his sleep."

He saw her eyes dancing. "We've had a terrific marriage."

"Then make sure you keep it. But do all of us a favor first—get horizontal for about eight hours before you make any decisions."

"But what if she's—"

"My bet is that she's fine, just doesn't want to be located now. You talked to her sister yet?"

"Yeah." Even through his fatigue, he'd heard the odd note in Belinda's voice, he realized now. "You're right. She knows something."

"Belinda will pay attention. And much as she loves her sister, she'll contact you first if something worries her. Let all of this go for a few hours, then cook up your plans."

"Don't suppose you'd like to clue me in on some good ideas?"

"Doc…" Her expression was withering. "I just smack some sense into you. Your courtin', well… You're on your own." She winked. "You musta been good at it once." She waved and walked off.

"Thanks, Stel. I mean it."

A nod, and she slipped back into the E.R.

Was he still capable of wooing his wife?

She'd been starry-eyed and romantic the first time.

This vanishing act told him she wouldn't be a soft touch now.

He shuffled down the hall like the old man he felt more often these days, his mind slogging through molasses.

Sleep first. And decent food.

The thought that she'd left him food cheered him. There had to be hope.

Hadn't there?

CHAPTER SEVEN

LILAH DROPPED the key to her sister's apartment and juggled grocery bags as she bent to retrieve it. Muttering, she balanced her purse on one hip and listened to Puddin' howl on the other side of the door.

When at last she opened it, the dog threw himself at her as if she'd trekked to the Gobi Desert since his last sight of her. "I know, baby, I know. You need to go out?"

She'd gotten far too accustomed to tapping a garage-door button and traversing only a few feet from car to kitchen counter. To possessing a large, beautiful yard where Puddin' could attend to the necessities at his leisure.

Her sister had never been so fortunate, even when she was married, and now her lot was much worse. This small apartment was all she could afford on spotty child-support payments and her salary. Lilah and Jake had offered to take Belinda and the kids in, but Belinda was proud and resolute.

And here Lilah was, making crowded living quarters only worse.

Maybe if her own marriage was over, she and

Belinda could share a house. She'd have to get serious about that catering business, but perhaps she'd be able to make her sister's life easier, as well.

The very notion of leaving her home, her nest, was sheer misery. And losing Jake—

Stop. Don't think like that. It won't help.

So Lilah would lose herself in a time-honored escape from life's rough passages.

She would cook. She was worn-out from a restless night, but she wasn't going to fall into the trap of sleep. It lured her like a lover, but its appeal was of the hiding-under-covers variety, and she had to resist. If her life with Jake was over—dear mercy, how she hoped not— then she had to stay on her feet.

Puddin' whimpered again. "Hang on, fella. Let me just put this milk in the fridge. There." She scanned the kitchen she'd already cleaned after Belinda and the kids had left, the laundry folded and put away. She had in mind to fill Belinda's freezer compartment, modest as it was, with some meals to reheat after a long day at work.

She'd prepare them a dinner to remember tonight, as well, and when they arrived, the rest of the apartment would be sparkling.

Maybe Lilah couldn't keep her husband's interest, but making a home, a refuge—this, she understood. There wasn't a lot her sister would allow her to do for her, but Lilah could stock her pantry and gift her with some leisure while she was here.

And it would take her mind off the man who was breaking her heart.

She plucked Puddin's leash from atop her suitcase. "Okay, boy. Here we go."

Lilah had no idea what her next step should be.

So she would just stay busy until she did.

JAKE PEERED INTO the mirror at the creases on his face from where he'd gone prostrate on the bed and apparently not moved an inch for hours.

What did Lilah see when she looked at this face? Damn, he was getting old. Gray at his temples—yeah, he'd rather say silver, but facts were facts—and not the hard, flat belly he'd had for most of his life. His was in better shape than a lot of his colleagues, but the resemblance to the man Lilah had married was not as strong as it had been.

He seldom gave a moment's thought to his appearance these days in more than an "I'm clean and everything's covered" sense. He'd been a natty dresser as a plastic surgeon, since appearances had been crucial to his practice, but he'd happily returned to the blue jeans of his youth after switching specialties. Trauma victims cared only about your competence, assuming they were conscious enough to notice.

He was older, yes, but he and Lilah had a terrific sex life anyway, thank goodness.

Or they once had.

Man, this introspection was killing him. He wasn't one for navel gazing, for processing his emotions or any of that psychobabble stuff.

But when you couldn't pin down precisely when

you'd last made love to your wife, that had to make a man reconsider. He felt a little as if he'd gone to sleep in one place and awakened on a foreign soil, the bedrock of his existence become quicksand.

He wanted his old life back. His old wife—though he was smart enough to wince at that phrase—back.

What about the traveling we were going to do?

Traveling was for retirement, wasn't it? For when you had nothing better?

The man in the mirror stared at him. *And just exactly what's better than making the person you love most happy?*

But first he had to find her. Get her to speak to him, though how he would do that…

Do you want lessons?

"I wonder, Stel," he grumbled. The steps he'd tried so far hadn't worked out so well.

Then his eyes went wide as a notion struck.

He crossed to the phone and dialed Belinda's number at work.

"This is Belinda. How may I help you?"

"I have an idea to win over Lilah."

A long pause. "Jake?"

"Well, hell, yes. Who else would it be?"

"You sound…better."

"I dropped into a dead sleep. Now I'm planning how to get my wife back."

"You found her?"

"Don't BS me, Bee. She's with you, I'd bet money."

"Um, I couldn't say."

"I understand I'm putting you in the middle. But I'm crazy about her, even if she did abandon me."

"Did she? Or was it you who ditched her first?"

"Ouch." He frowned. "Is that what she believes? Bee, I've been working my ass off to make a better life for us."

"You already had one to envy, Jake."

"But it was—" What? How did he explain the itch, the uneasy realization that what he'd accomplished hadn't really mattered? That he didn't have many years left to do so?

"Jake, I'm not the person you need to discuss this with."

"But Lilah left me. She doesn't want to talk."

She laughed. "Don't be such a guy. Of course she does."

"So why did she go?"

A hearty sigh. "Men are such idiots. I could have sworn you were different."

"I have news for you, honey. I am a guy."

"I guess so, but I just thought you got how to treat a woman. You're not impressing me lately, though, I have to say."

If her tone hadn't been so fond and teasing, he'd take umbrage, but Belinda was like his own little sister. And she was as close as he was likely to get to Lilah at the moment.

"Okay, knock off the insults and help me. This is for her own good."

"Sadly I believe that, so I'm prepared to rat out my own sister."

Jake pumped his fist. "Yes!"

"Don't start the victory dance yet. You have got some making up to do. Missing Our Day—are you kidding me?"

"I know, I know. I'm scum, I'm worthless—but damn it, Bee, I've been putting in a lot of hours."

"Yeah. Why?"

"Why? Because I'm needed."

"Lilah needs you, too."

He frowned. "Really?" She was always so in control, so on top of things. Of course she loved him, but... needed him?

Another sigh. "You truly do have a lot of talking to do. Have you not been listening to a word she says?"

"Why does she tell you these things and not me?"

"Jake, if you want my assistance, please don't keep revealing how dense you are. I mean, you've been my model, my hero. These feet of clay are killing me."

He struggled with temper and didn't speak.

"Okay, sorry. I love you and I'm not out to hurt your feelings or insult you, but honestly, Jake—you have to pay attention to you two as a couple. The kids are gone. You could be lying in bed together, making love for hours, traveling, doing a million things I may not live long enough to do. You've got the money, you're both healthy and you love each other, but instead of pulling together, you're drifting apart. Why are you not taking advantage of a situation other people would kill to have?"

"Wow." He blinked. "I have no clue what to say." This was so much bigger than he'd realized.

"Listen, I've got to get back to work. Anyway, you should be discussing this with Lilah."

"Wait—don't leave yet. Just—" He raked anxious fingers through his hair. "Look, I have an idea I want to try. Will you help me?"

"Does the idea include ditching your pager?"

"Ouch. It's that bad?"

"I'll refer you to the previous insults. Yes, things are that bad. And of course I'll help you, you big bozo. If I believed for a second that you didn't adore her, I wouldn't lift a finger, but I'm positive you do. Now, I really have to go. Text me on my cell, and she won't realize we're communicating if she's there."

"Bee—thanks. I mean it. I owe you."

"Just treasure my sister the way she deserves to be, okay? Then we'll be even."

"I love you, too, kid. You know that, right?"

"I do. Now, scram. Contact me when you've got things set up, and I'll do my part."

She disconnected.

Jake stood at the window for a long time. How had he not understood what was going on with the woman who was everything to him?

He replaced the receiver, then scrubbed his hands over his face and headed for the shower.

He had work to do. Plans to put in place.

CHAPTER EIGHT

"LILAH, THIS IS absolutely delicious—don't you agree, guys?" Belinda glanced at Thad and her daughter, Becky.

"Uh-huh. Wish you could cook like this, Mom." Thad spoke around a monster bite of the whole-grain focaccia-bread pizza Lilah had often used to trick her children into eating something healthy.

"Thad!" Lilah admonished. "Your mother is a wonderful cook."

"Not like you, big sis. Facts are facts."

Lilah peered into Belinda's face, but her sister seemed unperturbed. "I don't have a full-time job or—" Sliding her gaze to first one child, then the other, she tried to indicate the responsibility Belinda bore pretty much single-handedly.

Belinda shrugged. "Even if I had all day, I wouldn't spend it in the kitchen. You have a gift, Lilah, and you love it."

"I'd better. I may have to support myself with it." Lilah ignored her sister's instant distress. "I was wondering…" She kept her tone carefully casual. "How would you feel about sharing a house?"

"Lilah! You can't be serious." She leaned closer and whispered, "Your marriage is not over."

The melancholy that had swooped in the second she'd washed the last pot hovered once more. "I'm not so certain. Jake loves what he's doing. Who am I to rob him of it?"

"You can't give up." Belinda's voice was harsh. "If you'd only—"

"What are you two whispering about?" Becky's eyes narrowed. "Why do you seem so sad, Aunt Lilah?"

Whatever Bee had been about to say would have to wait. "I'm fine, honey—I promise. Just a little tired. So—" She brightened her tone. "How did your report on dolphins go?"

As her niece began to speak, Lilah forced her mind away from all thoughts of Jake. Whatever would happen in her marriage, well, she'd face it. But this child in front of her had been suffering from her parents' divorce for months now. Here was something constructive she could do.

Carefully she drew Becky out on one point of her topic, then another, and the normally shy girl turned eager. When they'd exhausted the subject, Lilah moved to the next phase of her plans from this morning. "Kids, would you let me help you with homework tonight and put you to bed? I'd like to keep you all to myself for a little bit."

Becky frowned. So did Thad. "But what about Mom?"

"I was remembering that your mom loves books, and wondering if she might like to make a little trip to the bookstore. Have herself a coffee, read a magazine or two, just…have the night off."

Both children studied their mother curiously. "You need a night off?"

Lilah laughed. "Every mom could use a break now and again. Your uncle Jake used to shoo me out of the house sometimes for that very same purpose." She bit her lip at the bittersweet memory.

"When's Uncle Jake going to be here? Doesn't he miss you?" Becky asked.

Lilah and Belinda traded glances. Lilah's throat tightened.

Belinda rode to the rescue. "Of course he does. We're just borrowing Aunt Lilah for a bit." A sideways look was pregnant with meaning, except Lilah couldn't translate. "She'll be going home soon, so we'd better enjoy her while we've got her, right?"

"Yeah—and her cooking," offered Thad.

"Absolutely. And the housekeeping, I might add." Belinda sent her a warm smile, and Lilah was relieved that Belinda had taken no offense. "Thank you again for all you did today. But I can't let you work tonight, too."

Lilah smiled wistfully. "You forget that I've done all this before." She faced the kids. "I miss having a houseful. I'd like to keep them, if you'd let me."

"Sure!" said Thad. "But you can't tickle."

Lilah's eyebrows rose. "Wanna bet?"

The boy beamed.

"Mama, you should go," said Becky with the maturity that had evolved as their little family had broken up. "We'll be fine."

Belinda was obviously conflicted.

"Go ahead. Enjoy yourself."

"Oh, I will, but—" She bent to her children, one on each side, and hugged them, planting a big kiss on each of them. "I'll miss you two monkeys." Her eyes glistened.

Lilah's own were moist. "We'll be fine. Now scram." She waggled her eyebrows at Becky and Thad. "We have some mischief to get into." She rubbed her hands together. How long it had been! "After homework, of course."

Belinda emerged from her bedroom, buttoning her coat. She withdrew her cell phone from her purse and glanced down, forehead wrinkled.

"What?" Lilah rose and stepped away from the children. "Are you all right?"

Belinda snapped her phone shut. "Yes—sure. Absolutely." She kissed her kids once more, then hustled to the door, a secret smile on her face. Almost as an afterthought, she turned back. "Thank you again, Lilah. I'll be back soon."

"No rush."

Belinda appeared so pleased that Lilah was delighted.

Except, her sister seemed almost too satisfied. Perhaps there was a man in her life. If so, Lilah couldn't be happier.

Even if she wanted to cry over her own lost love.

LILAH JERKED AWAKE when the apartment door opened. "Hey," she greeted her sister. "How was it?"

Belinda busied herself hanging up her coat. "Great. Thank you so mu—" The last word was swallowed up in a huge yawn. "Sorry. How were the kids?"

"Wonderful, of course. You've got two sweethearts there, Bee. You should be proud of them—and yourself."

Belinda's face crumpled. "You can't imagine what that means. I worry all the time—are they getting enough attention because I have to work and I'm so blasted tired all the time? Am I handling all this the best way? I just—" She pressed her lips together. "I long to give them the world, but I can barely make the rent."

Lilah embraced her sister and rocked slowly, stroking circles on Belinda's back. "You're doing a terrific job with them. They'll be fine, I swear. And if we move in together, I'll help you out."

Belinda tensed slightly. "Lilah—"

"But we won't fret over any of that tonight," Lilah assured her. "You go get some sleep. I'll lock up."

A quick squeeze, and Belinda let go. "Thanks so much—oh. I forgot. I brought the kids a surprise, but I left it in the car. I'll just go get it—"

"Let me." Lilah stopped her with a hand on her arm. "You have to work tomorrow. Go on to bed."

Belinda frowned. "You must be tired, too, after all you did today."

"I managed a catnap. I'm good." Lilah snagged Belinda's car keys from the outside pocket of her purse. "Sweet dreams."

"Lilah—"

She halted at the note in her sister's voice. "What?"

Belinda bit her lip. "Nothing. Just—I love you."

Lilah smiled. "I love you, too." Then she was out the door.

The chill wind kicked up, and Lilah bundled her jacket more closely, her mind on solutions to her sister's dilemma. She threaded her way between cars, searching for where Belinda had parked—

A big hand grabbed her shoulder; another clapped over her mouth.

She yelped, began to struggle.

"Lilah, don't. It's okay. It's me."

Jake?

Then she was spun around, too swiftly to register anything—

But his lips on hers. A kiss unlike any she'd had in— Ever.

Her heart fluttered. He felt so wonderful. So familiar and dear.

She broke away. "What are you doing here?"

That slashing grin that had charmed her for too many years still wielded magic. "Coming for you." Before she could react, he swung her into his arms and strode across the pavement.

"Wait—I can't. Belinda—"

"Is right behind you," said another familiar voice. "My keys, please?"

Lilah glanced between the two of them. Glared at her. "Traitor."

Belinda shrugged. "You two needed to talk."

"I've tried that." Lilah started to struggle again.

But Jake had always been strong—and now he was determined. "Uh-uh, lover. Just hand her the keys."

Lilah closed her fingers tightly around them and hugged them to her chest. "Why should I?"

"Because I'm bigger." But in the glow of the mercury vapor lamps, she saw what she couldn't before—that he was more worried than his confident tone would convey.

Her heart skipped just a little. Had she finally gotten through to him?

"Bully," she grumbled without heat.

"Harpy." But he grinned. "Please, Lilah." He looked sideways at Belinda, then bent nearer. "I have plans. I think you'll like them." A pause. "At least, I hope you will."

Wasn't his focus fully on her as she'd wished for so long? Didn't she love him to distraction?

Yes and yes.

But would anything change, really? To be hesitant to trust this man was horrible, but the fear was real. "This isn't a game, Jake."

His brown eyes had never been softer. Sadder. "I know."

Their gazes held for endless moments. She was terrified at the distance she felt.

He was a good man. He was here. Shouldn't that count?

She realized he'd read her doubts, was about to set her down. Abruptly she decided. "Here—" She tossed the keys to her sister without a backward glance.

Threw her arms around his neck and buried her face in his throat.

For a second, he bowed his head to hers, and she felt him shudder. "Thank God."

She thought she heard him tell her sister goodbye, but she paid attention to nothing but the feel of this man she'd missed so much, the scent that had accompanied her into dreams for the better part of her life.

And when he settled her into the passenger seat of his car, she clung for a moment before letting go.

"God, babe, I am so sorry," he said.

He kissed her again, then rounded the car.

SHE SEEMED SMALL, sitting there in the other seat. He had several inches on her, but her personality was so oversized that she always appeared bigger.

What he wouldn't do for his old Chevy with the bench seat in front, so they could drive plastered against each other as they'd done when they first dated.

He couldn't tell what she was thinking. Why she was so quiet. He had no idea if she'd like the place he'd found. If he'd brought the right clothes for her.

He hadn't recognized some of the underwear. The notion that they dressed together so seldom that he didn't even know she'd bought new lingerie had hit him hard.

What else had he missed about her?

"Where are we going?" she asked.

Suddenly he remembered a step of his plan he'd omitted. He steered to the shoulder of the road, then felt like a fool and almost didn't stop.

"What is it?"

He summoned a smile. Waggled his eyebrows as though he actually felt playful. "Turn around."

"What?" She frowned.

"I skipped a step. Look out the side window."

She stared at him for a second, and he faltered. "Never mind." He reached for the steering wheel, but she grabbed his hand.

Granted him a tiny smile, then faced the door as he'd asked.

He hesitated, less sure of himself than he'd been since high school.

But she was here, and she was going along with him. For both their sakes, he had to conquer his nerves and pull this off. He drew the scarf from his pocket, looped it over her head and fastened it around her eyes, tying it as carefully as he'd ever knotted a suture.

The hitch in her breathing got to him.

He pressed a kiss to that sensitive juncture of neck and shoulder to remind them both of better days.

A gasp gave him hope. His tongue slicked over her in a slow, heated lick.

She shivered.

He smiled against her skin. Barely resisted the urge to swing her around and crush her to him.

But this was a seduction. He would go slow if it killed both of them.

Which felt entirely possible.

"Sit back." He breathed the words over her flesh and watched her shiver again. Then he drew out the second scarf gently and tied her wrists together. "Trust me, love," he said, and traced his tongue over her lips. "Please."

She swallowed visibly. Her mouth parted just a little.

Jake had to restrain himself from clutching her to him again, but he managed. Shifted back into his seat.

And drove into the night.

CHAPTER NINE

THE CAR STOPPED.

She didn't know where they were. How long they'd traveled in silence. The air practically zinged with nerves.

She hadn't felt like this even the first night they'd made love, though she'd certainly been off balance. Her eagerness back then had overcome any anxiety except whether he'd find her beautiful.

He'd been gorgeous. Lanky and with the pallor of a med student who spent all his time indoors studying, though he'd been an avid cyclist before his life got swallowed up in his calling.

They'd both been dead broke, and his apartment was more of a hovel, a small space in the attic of an old house near the university.

She hadn't cared one whit. She'd been in love, crazy over him. Positive that they belonged together.

But now, she had no idea where they were or what he intended. He'd blindfolded her. Seized control.

However adventurous their sex life had been, this was somehow different. *He* was different.

The door snicked open. She had the sense of light at the edges of her blindfold, quickly shuttered by the closing of the door.

Then she waited. Yearned. Her skin literally ached for his touch.

Suddenly her seat belt vanished. His arms slipped beneath her bottom, behind her back. Lifted her, then whirled around and around until she was dizzy.

Jake, she almost said, but she didn't want to disturb… whatever this was.

Amazing, for sure. Arousing, yes, unbelievably so. To be helpless in the arms of a man you knew and loved but couldn't predict—

She shivered. Moaned. Let her head fall back in abandon. Felt him nuzzle inside her bodice, his warmth electrifying, the sharp edge of promise unnerving…delicious.

She craved more. She was half out of her mind with longing to touch him. To torture him as he—

A hum deep in his chest, a very sexy growl. The wet shock of his tongue trailing a path down the valley between her breasts.

She arched. All but writhed. "Jake." She lifted her bound hands helplessly. "Let me see."

"Uh-uh" was the reply as he licked his way toward her nipple.

And as he did, he began walking. Her feet bumped something solid. "Sorry," he mumbled.

"Where are we?"

"That's for me to know and you to find out," he

said. The arm beneath her thighs twisted, then she heard a door open.

And slam once they were through. Jake strode with her across a wide space. She heard metal clicks, then felt the cool night breeze again.

Finally he set her down. Untied her wrists and removed her coat. Wrapped his arms around her waist. "I'll keep you warm," he murmured. Then his breath whispered against her throat, his mouth cruising over her skin while his hands traveled her body. Fingers dipped inside the waistband of her jeans, tore at the snap, pulled down the zipper.

She gasped. "Jake—" If she didn't get her hands on him, she'd die.

"Not yet." Those long fingers glided over her belly, up beneath her bra, then around until the hooks were unfastened, her breasts were freed—

Cool night air kissed her flesh as her jeans slid down her legs, her shirt buttons opened—

Then Lilah was naked. Outside. In the night.

With no way to know whether they were alone or someone was watching. Never in her life had she felt anything like this.

She trembled with the thrill of it.

Then his jeans pressed to her bare bottom. Lilah gasped, and squirmed against him. "Jake—" She was nearly whimpering now.

His fingers were everywhere, teasing a gossamer trail over her navel and down—

They slipped inside her, and she lost it. Came, violently.

"Good." His voice was strained but proud. "Remember me. Remember us, Lilah."

She heard the rasp of his zipper, then felt the heat of him against her. He bent his knees, spread her legs. Thrust inside in a long, smooth stroke.

Lilah's breath caught. They both stilled. Jake held her close. "Lilah…" Husky, desperate, his voice was so dear that tears sprang to her eyes.

She lifted her arms, first one, then the second. Wrapped them around his neck. She wanted to turn in his arms nearly as much as she feared breaking the spell.

Then Jake began to move, and all thought fled. Seeking fingers, the scrape of teeth, the lick of his tongue…all played harmony to the driving beat of him inside her, so beloved yet so new. She undulated against him, relishing every second of the shock, the surprise, the forbidden.

"I love you," he murmured. "Love you so."

Before she could respond, he fastened his teeth to her vulnerable nape—

She soared and he joined her. Stars burst behind her eyes.

Silence pulsed between them. Then he spoke. "Lilah, I'm so sorry." Breathing heavily, he gripped her with near desperation. Buried his face in her hair. "Don't leave me. You are my love."

Her throat thick with sobs, Lilah twisted in the arms of the man she'd adored for more than half of her life. Cradled his face in her hands, and kissed him with all the tenderness in her heart. "I love you, too." She wrapped her arms around his neck and held on.

She wept.

And Jake's broad shoulders shook.

WHEN SHE AWOKE, they were tangled together as they once were every night.

But this time Jake was staring as if memorizing every cell of her. His eyes were sorrowful. Serious, even when he smiled to greet her. "Hey."

"Hey." Her voice was hoarse. He'd made her scream, actually scream. She stroked his jaw. "You all right?"

"I'm not sure. You?"

She felt shy, awkward, so she dodged. "That was amazing." She blinked. "What got into you?"

"You have to ask?" He covered his own discomfort with a grin.

Jake was no more adept at discussing his feelings than any other man, but she couldn't allow that, not now. Too much was on the line. "I do. Talk to me, Jake."

He glanced away, then back. Frowned. "What's happened between us, Lilah? Were you really going to leave me?"

"I didn't want to. I just couldn't figure out what else to do."

"Because of Our Day? I told you I was sorry. I sent you roses. I said I'd clean the mess up."

"You did," she said, her voice as heavy as her heart.

"What's wrong? You didn't like the roses, did you?"

She raised the sheet, clutched it to her chest.

"Don't."

"Don't what?"

"Hide from me." He pulled her back down, shoved the sheet away. "This is me, damn it. We don't conceal ourselves from each other—at least, we never used to."

"Once we didn't do lots of things—" She halted.

"Keep going. Like what?"

Then she got mad. Sat up, scooted around to face him. "We didn't spend most nights apart. Sleep in separate beds."

"We do not." He sat up, too.

She poked him in the chest. "What do you call the couch in the study, huh? Do you know have any idea how many times you haven't come to bed?"

"I was trying not to disturb you—"

"You jerk." She leaped from the bed. "I never rest without you. I don't like sleeping alone." She started pacing. "You used to be married to me, not the E.R."

"What?" He followed her. "You're kidding me. Lilah, I'm just doing my job—"

"You had a job! You left it—left *me*. Flipped our lives upside down. You turned into an adrenaline junkie, and pretty soon, you didn't need me anymore."

He recoiled. "Is that what you think?"

She shoved her hair back from her tear-swollen face. "You weren't like this before. I just don't understand why I keep coming up short to your new mistress. What your work gives you that I can't."

He stood in the center of the room, gaping at her. "Lilah, you understood why I made the switch."

She shook her head. "I don't. We had plans, Jake, dreams we'd talked about for years. All of a sudden you've sold your practice, and despite the fact that we have plenty of money, you don't choose to spend that time with me after all. Instead you decide to go into trauma where you'll never have to see me."

"That's not fair. I love you. Why would I avoid you?" He closed the distance. "I don't spend much more time away than I did in my practice, it's just different hours."

"You're wrong. You're gone all the time, and I'm—"

"What?" He clasped her arms. "Lonely?"

She blinked hard. Tried to get away.

He wouldn't let her. "You're missing the kids, aren't you? They kept you incredibly busy, but now the nest is empty."

She poked his chest. "Don't you patronize me. I don't need my kids to make me complete—" She glared. "Maybe I don't need you, either—" She yanked away.

But Jake sensed that he had to keep her near, maintain physical contact in order to work through this.

"Let me go. I'd like to get dressed."

"That's not a good idea, babe."

"Release me, Jake."

"No can do." Instead he swept her up, carried her not to the bed but to a big overstuffed rocking chair in the corner.

She fought him a little, but he had the advantage and used it. "You want to talk? Fine, but you'll stay right here to do it."

"Then I'm getting dressed." She hunched in his lap.

"What?"

"I don't like being naked with you."

"Why?" He was honestly shocked.

She kept her eyes cast down. "I'm not pretty anymore."

"Get real." He chuckled. "Of course you are. Beautiful as ever."

"Don't make light of this."

The pain on her face wiped away his smile. He couldn't let her put distance—or clothes—between them again. He was forced to peel her open, though, curled like a shrimp as she was. "Lilah, I have watched you give birth to our babies, I've held your hair while you tossed your cookies, I've been naked with you in nearly every way possible and I just made love to you— pretty fiercely, I might add—when you were only a few minutes younger than you are now. What on earth do you possibly have to hide from me?"

"I don't know." She kept her arms wrapped tightly around herself. "I just don't— I wish I were still young and everything was smooth and taut."

He cuddled her and started rocking. "You think I don't feel the same about myself?"

She snorted. "Guys don't sag this soon."

"Lilah, I loved you young and I love you—"

Her head lifted. Her eyes narrowed. "You weren't going to say old."

"Of course not." He hazarded another grin. "Do I look stupid?"

When her mouth twitched, he had the urge to celebrate, but they weren't nearly through yet. "Stella says I'm a fool. And not indispensable."

No reaction.

"I never believed I was. I just liked—" He puzzled over it a minute. "Being needed."

"Yeah," she said.

He glanced down. "I never thought you needed me, not really."

Her eyes went wide. "What?"

"Lilah, you've been juggling a house and kids and husband and pets and every committee known to man—you take my breath away at all you tackle and how easy you make it seem. You're the most capable person I've ever met."

"Really?"

"What on earth have I been doing that you don't realize that?"

"But you're the one who has the tough job. Even before trauma."

"Are you kidding me? I have nurses and administrators and techs—there's a whole team to support my every move. You tackle the world single-handed and whip it into shape daily."

They stared at each other. "I had no idea," she said. Then she sat up as though unaware of her nudity. "You admire me." She seemed stunned.

"Lilah, I love you."

She waved that off. "That's different. Admiration means respect."

He gaped. "If I haven't convinced you before now

that I not only adore you but respect you, no wonder you were leaving me."

She ducked her head. "It broke my heart, but I couldn't figure out how else to get your attention." Then she captured his gaze. "I didn't marry our kids or our house or our social position, Jake. I married you, the man who was deep in debt for student loans, who lived off ramen noodles and rode a bike because he couldn't afford a car. The possessions that accompanied your success were gravy. I love our kids, of course, but I juggled all of that because it was us. Me and you, a team. And we were supposed to get to be a couple again when the kids left, but instead Bob died, and you left, too."

"Bob? What's he got to do with it?"

"After his death, you changed. Almost overnight, you sold your practice, went into trauma. It's like you became possessed."

He drew her closer. Shook his head against the tumble of her hair. "Honey, I never meant to desert you. You're right—losing Bob really made me reevaluate. It's hard to accept that your time on earth is finite. I wanted my life to mean something. To make a difference to more than vain women."

"I understand, I do. But isn't there some way to have that and still have a life together? I would never ask you to give up work you love, but I'm—" She bit her lip. Glanced away.

He grasped her chin and made her face him. "You're what?"

"Scared," she whispered. "I don't want to lose you, and you're killing yourself right before my eyes."

He wasn't as shocked as he might have been. *Have you studied the schedule lately?* "I may be too old for trauma." He couldn't believe he'd just admitted his worst fear. "But I'm not ready to be useless, Lilah."

"Oh, Jake…" She cupped his jaw. "We can't help aging, but that doesn't mean we don't have contributions to make." She kissed him softly. "I'm just greedy for every last day with you I can get."

He placed his hand over hers. "I'm realizing that I've been pressing to keep up with people who are twenty years younger. I haven't wanted to admit I'm finding it difficult."

Her smile was sympathy and understanding. "So what do we do now?"

"I'm not sure, exactly." He pondered. "I could definitely begin by only working the shifts that are on the schedule. I couldn't cut back yet without burdening the rest of them, but—" He locked his gaze on hers. "If I have to go back to plastics, I will, Lilah. Nothing's worth losing you."

Tears rolled down her cheeks. "You won't. We can figure this out, as long as we're talking. I just— I miss you, Jake."

She folded into his arms, fitting perfectly as she always had. "I miss you, too." He kissed the top of her head. "I am so sorry about Our Day, honey. I'm going to make it up to you, I swear. As a matter of fact—" He scooted to the front of the rocker and rose with her still in his arms. "Let me show you part of how I planned to do it."

He walked into the living room of the cottage he'd

had to beg from a colleague. "Close your eyes." He set her down and began lighting candles. "No peeking."

He noticed her shiver but wasn't eager to leave her long enough to get their suitcases. He snatched an afghan from the sofa and wrapped her in it, keeping his arms around her, too. "Okay."

She opened them, and he tried to see it all through her eyes, the table set for two, the golden glow reflected in crystal and silver, exotic blossoms of gardenia and mimosa, bird of paradise and calla lilies spilling over the center of the table.

"Oh, Jake…"

"The champagne should still be cold, even if the ice is melted. I meant to woo you first, not ravish you."

Her head tilted to his. "I liked being ravished."

"Yeah?"

"A definite wow." She revolved in his arms. Let the afghan drop. "As a matter of fact…"

"Oh, babe, don't look at me like that."

"Okay." Instead she rose to her toes and didn't look at him at all. She was too busy kissing him, stroking him.

"We're not going to get any cold champagne at this rate."

"I don't care." She trailed kisses across his jaw, down his throat.

"Um, is there anything else we should talk about first?"

"Uh-uh," she murmured as her mouth traveled lower.

"So…we're good? You're not leaving—" he gasped as her lips did wicked things to him "—me?"

She paused in her torture. "We're good." She smiled the old Lilah smile, the one that told him all was right with the world. "Real good." She winked, then returned to her task.

His eyes nearly rolled back in his head. "Lilah—"

Before he lost it completely, he bent, scooped her up. Grabbed the champagne on his way to the bed. "It's after midnight. Happy Valentine's Day, my love."

Lilah laughed. Shifted and clamped her legs around his waist.

He stumbled, nearly dropped the bottle and her both.

But he wouldn't, not again. He'd almost lost her. She was his woman, the best part of his life. He was here to stay.

And she wasn't running anywhere. "By the way, forget the circus," he murmured against her lips. "Unless you take me with you."

She chuckled. Kissed him hard.

And held on tight.

* * * * *

Dear Reader,

Many years ago, as a lonely expatriate newly arrived in Germany, I took my three-year-old daughter to a playground as a respite from the hotel room we were living in until we found a home. It was early morning, and the only other visitors were a mother and two little boys. She and I struck up a conversation that day that was the beginning of a lifelong friendship. During that first autumn she introduced me to her family, her village and her life as a vintner in the Riesling wine region called the Rheingau. It was my memories of the time I spent on her hillside vineyards and in her centuries-old wine cellar that became the starting point for the story you are about to read.

In writing for—and reading—the Harlequin Everlasting Love stories, I've been struck by how intensely personal they are. The emphasis in tales of lifelong love is *life*—its joys, its disappointments, its celebrations and rituals, its acknowledgment of what is good and true and essential. I love writing about everlasting love, and I hope that you will love reading—about real love and real life. I'd also love to hear from you about your own "everlasting love." Please write to me at P.O. Box 298, Enfield, CT 06083-0298 or linda@lindacardillo.com.

With warm wishes,

Linda Cardillo

THE HAND THAT
GIVES THE ROSE

Linda Cardillo

To Stephan, my own everlasting love

Acknowledgment

I am so grateful to my friend Ursula von Breitenbach, who not only taught me how to harvest grapes and judge a fine Riesling vintage, but also renewed my creative spirit with long weekends devoted to painting and poetry (and more Riesling). My special thanks also to Kasia Novak, whose memories of childhood summers in Warsaw added vibrancy and richness to my research.

To the friends and family who have supported me along the way, I also offer a warm thank-you—especially to Betsy Port, who cheered me on with infectious enthusiasm; Lani Kretschmar, who listened to my daily musings and plottings and lent her keen eye to proofreading; Toni Robinson, who spread the word far and wide to her network; and to my sister, Cindy McLaughlin, and my cousins Joan Cito, Mari Adele Thomas and Gene Vetrano, who were my "street team."

"The fragrance always stays in the hand that gives the rose."

—Hada Bejar

PROLOGUE

MARIELLE HARTMANN was an only child, although this didn't become significant to her until later in life. When she was a little girl, her father, a great bear of a man, would carry her on his shoulders up the dirt road that led to their vineyards. She clutched his hands, giant paws that held her securely as they climbed higher and higher. She could smell the musty, sweet aroma of fermenting grapes that clung to his thick curly hair and she could feel his heart beating steadily beneath her legs. When they reached the top of the hill, he spun her around in a whirling jig and she watched their acres and acres of vines spin with her, their gray-green leaves lifting in the breeze and their fruit pendulous and full of promise.

"Taste this," he said, as he thrust his hand through a tangle of broad leaves and emerged with a perfect cluster of grapes. He held them out to her in his palm, tiny pale globes of translucent green. She felt like a princess then, being offered a treasure of pearls as she surveyed her kingdom.

Behind them the Taunus Mountains formed a barrier against the cold north wind, and below them the Rhine River was a slate-blue ribbon warming the soil of their southern-facing slopes. This particular geography had made it possible for her family to grow grapes for more than three centuries in a region of Germany that was as far north as Saskatchewan. She understood that only later. As a child, this land was her playground, not her livelihood. It was the earth upon which she learned her father's love.

And as a woman, it was the ground upon which Tomas Marek first stepped into her life.

CHAPTER ONE

October 1975

THE CLANG OF Marielle Hartmann's alarm clock ricocheted off the walls of the bedroom that had been hers as a girl. She reached out from under the down comforter her mother had retrieved from a trunk two days before and turned off the insistent bell. She could see through the slender cracks in the ancient shutters that it was still dark outside. 4:00 a.m. Marielle reminded herself that she was no longer in Frankfurt as she looked around the room she had not inhabited in nearly eight years.

She stretched her arms over her head and threw her long legs over the side of the bed and onto the cold stone floor. She could hear her mother already in the kitchen, so she grabbed her things and headed to the bathroom. Anita wouldn't be pleased if Marielle was late for the first day of the wine harvest.

Instead of the conservative navy suit she usually wore to her job as an economist at Deutsche Bank,

Marielle pulled on a pair of jeans, a flannel shirt and a pair of thick wool socks before joining her mother downstairs.

Anita handed her a mug of coffee and Marielle could see that she'd brewed a full urn to take out to the vineyards for the harvest crew.

"How was Papa's night?" Marielle asked as she sipped the steaming coffee, waiting for the jolt of caffeine she needed to start her day.

Anita shook her head. Marielle could see the fatigue in her mother's eyes, the stoop in her shoulders. She berated herself for not noticing sooner the toll her father's stroke was taking on her mother when she'd come to visit in July. Late in the evening during that visit—after her father, Max, had been settled in bed for the night—Marielle had sat with Anita and a bottle of their vineyard's best wine.

Anita had uncorked it with her usual expertise and poured a taste into one of the two gold-stemmed glasses etched with her family's name and crest. She'd set them out on the polished wood of a table in the winery's tasting room. The winery had been in Anita's family for over three hundred years. Anita herself, along with her parents and Max, had brought the vineyards back from the devastation of World War II. In the thirty years since the end of the war, she'd rescued fallow fields, planting new vines with her own hands, nurturing them through too much rain or not enough, protecting them from disease and finally, reaping the harvest of a unique Riesling that was only now gaining appreciation from wine connoisseurs. Until this spring, Max had been her partner in the enterprise—a man with a nose and a knack for viniculture and winemaking. It was Max who'd come to understand and love the land and the grapes it produced.

Marielle remembered trudging through the vineyards as a little girl, racing to keep up with her father as he inspected vines and scooped up handfuls of earth to test its acidity and moisture.

Although Marielle had followed her father around in the vineyards, it was Anita's example that she'd absorbed and found fascinating. In the afternoons, as she'd sat at the dining table doing homework, Anita had shared the workspace with her, managing the difficult decisions about staffing and equipment purchases and production, setting prices and courting customers. Marielle discovered her talent not only for math in those hours with Anita, but also for negotiating, sometimes helping her calculate prices and often listening to her bargain with suppliers. When Marielle had scored highly on the *Abitur,* the qualifying exam for university, she was offered a place in economics at the University of Mannheim, one of the best in the country.

With Max and Anita's blessing, she'd left home to pursue her studies and create a life for herself in the business world after graduating with honors from Mannheim. Marielle had flourished. At twenty-seven, she was one of only a few female vice presidents at Deutsche Bank. She'd spent two years in Hong Kong and had returned just three months ago.

It was while she was away that Max's grasp of wine-making and of his world had been obliterated in an instant by a stroke. He was no longer able to walk or speak, and had made little progress with his rehabilitation. Although she'd been shocked by the change in her father and his utter dependence upon Anita, Marielle had been both unable and unwilling to acknowledge what Max's condition meant for all of them—until that evening in July when Anita had poured her the wine.

"Taste it, *schatz*. Give me your opinion."

"It's excellent, Mama. One of the best, I think."

Anita nodded. "At least you can recognize a good vintage. It's a start." She rubbed her forehead, creased with new lines.

"A start of what?"

"You becoming a vintner."

Marielle sat very still. She'd known deep in her heart that her parents—especially her mother—would want her to inherit the winery. But that was decades away. Her second career. Something she planned after she'd made a name for herself in finance.

"Aren't you rushing things a little? You and Papa still have half a lifetime to spend running the business."

"No, Marielle, we don't." Anita gazed straightforwardly across the table at Marielle. Anita had never been one to tell Marielle fairy tales when she was a little girl. Storytelling had been Max's role. Anita was the realist, the practical housekeeper who knew exactly how much food she needed to buy when they opened the winery courtyard in summer for wine-tasting dinners; who knew which harvest crews were the best; who'd calculated to the penny the cost of producing every bottle of wine.

"We have no time left at all. Papa can't take part in the business. In fact, he can't be left alone anymore. In May, while I was up in the vineyards supervising the pruning, he fell out of bed. I won't put him in a home. But I cannot care for him *and* manage the business."

Marielle stared at her mother, trying to absorb the enormity of what she was saying, trying to deny what she knew her mother was about to ask her.

"I need you *now,* Marielle. Not in twenty or even ten years. I need you to come home. To carry on for me, for us."

Marielle could not answer at first. Her hand gripped the fragile stem of the wineglass with such intensity that it would have shattered if Anita hadn't gently loosened her fingers.

"I know this isn't what you expected for your life right now, to come back to this little village and a life dictated by the seasons after you've been racing across Southeast Asia making deals. But it's not what I expected for mine, either."

Anita sat erect, carrying her responsibilities with uncomplaining acceptance. It was what she'd always done. And it was what Marielle knew was expected of her, as well.

AND SO, IN THE WEEKS that followed, Marielle submitted her resignation at the bank and sublet her apartment, wrapping up the loose ends of her life in Frankfurt in time to be here with her mother on this first morning of the harvest.

CHAPTER TWO

THIN WISPS OF SMOKE curled from the rusted chimney pipes of the circled campers at the river's edge camping ground. The shadows of bodies stretching and pulling on shirts and sweaters indicated that the men inside were readying themselves for the day.

Marielle steered her mother's old Volkswagen bus off the B43 highway that ran along the Rhine where it jogged westward a little north of Mainz. She pulled into the campground and turned off the engine. She considered knocking at the door of Janosch Kosakowski's camper to let the crew chief know she'd arrived, but she had no idea which of the ancient metal boxes was his. She decided to wait for the men to emerge and tucked her hands inside her pockets to warm them.

The fog was still thick, hovering just above the water and seeping across the campground, the highway, and then up into the village and the vineyard-covered hillsides above it. The yellow lantern lights within the campers were the only warmth in this gray predawn morning.

Marielle tapped her foot impatiently and watched

her breath, wishing she'd thought to take a thermos of coffee with her. She pulled her woolen hat down over her ears and blew on her rapidly chilling fingers. She was about to start banging on every camper when the door to the middle one opened and two men stepped out. The first Marielle recognized as Janosch, the Pole who'd led the harvest crew for her family's vineyards for the past ten years. Behind him, stooping to clear the doorway, followed a lanky, dark-haired younger man.

As if Janosch had given a signal, the doors of the other campers opened and within five minutes six more men stood stomping in a muddy circle around him. He spoke a few words in Polish, gestured toward the Volkswagen and led the others toward Marielle.

She got out of the car as they approached and held out her hand to Janosch.

"Greetings! Welcome back."

Janosch reached up to pull off his woolen cap and smiled expansively. Marielle's impatience dissipated as she recognized familiar faces. Janosch introduced each member of the crew and they nodded silently or smiled and saluted as he rattled off their names. The last was the tall man who'd shared Janosch's camper. He barely acknowledged Marielle as Janosch announced his name. "Tomas Marek," he said. "Son of my sister."

Marielle opened the VW doors and waved the eight men in, breathing in the aromas of cheap Eastern European cigarettes and fried onions that had saturated the fabric of their jackets. She backed up the bus and headed out of the campground and up to the Hartmann vineyards on the hillside known as Johannisberg—St. John's Mountain. According to legend, it was Charlemagne who'd recognized the potential of this fragment of the Holy Roman Empire and had ordered the first vines planted.

The thing Marielle immediately noticed about Tomas Marek was his hands—pale, slender fingers in a pair of black wool gloves with the tips cut off. They were the hands of a musician, a violinist perhaps, or an artist used to handling delicate brushes. They were hands unmarked by weather or rough work, hands that had not lifted heavy crates of wine bottles, hands that hadn't tilled or planted or pruned. For Marielle, Tomas Marek's hands were both beautiful and useless.

Right now they were hands that he shoved into his pockets as he stood on the periphery of the harvest crew while Marielle demonstrated in a mixture of German, limited Polish and gestures what she expected of the crew on this first morning.

She'd listened to Anita give these directions for years—to her as a schoolgirl released from the classroom to work the harvest, and later whenever she could spare time from the bank to help her parents bring in the crop. But before she'd always been the listener, not the one giving directions. Marielle struggled within herself to set the tone of authority that Anita projected.

"Let them know from the beginning what you expect," Anita had advised. "Hard work, consistent effort, a steady pace, no rotten clusters to augment their baskets. For the most part, they'll work hard. Janosch knows how to put together a good crew—but watch out for newcomers who are either too inexperienced or too lazy to do the job well."

Marielle scanned the somber faces in the misty chill, the men's feet damp and shifting as she spoke. Who among them could she trust to follow instructions, work quickly and competently? Who among them might fail her? They were generally a sturdy group, with knowledge of the task. But her eyes and her doubts kept returning to Tomas Marek, who stood on the edge. He had lit a cigarette and barely listened to her, staring off at nothing since the fog hadn't yet lifted in the valley.

Rather than walk the row as the crew started to pick, Marielle decided to work alongside Tomas for a few hours so she could gauge his skill. She watched him finish his cigarette and crush it under the sole of his shoe. Like the rest of the crew he wore a shoddy Eastern European imitation of Adidas sport shoes, and they were already soaked through from the wet grass. Marielle's own feet were still snug in their sturdy Wellingtons, and she remembered hiking Mt. Kenya a few years earlier and being struck by the meager footwear of her guide. He'd worn thin-soled leather street shoes yet picked his way nimbly over the soggy, porous lower elevations and later the rocky trail as they approached the summit.

Like the Kenyan guide, Tomas seemed oblivious to the incongruity or discomfort of his shoes. He settled into a crouch and began snipping clusters of Riesling grapes from the lower branches of the vines, reaching behind the curtain of dripping leaves to interior clusters that a less experienced or lazy picker would have ignored. His long fingers deftly cradled a bunch in his left hand and he snapped his shears swiftly and cleanly over the stem. He withdrew his arm from the vine, gently placed the bunch of grapes in the canvas basket at his side, then moved back in for the next cluster. He worked with a steady, graceful rhythm, from the bottom to the top of the stalk, breaking the flow of his movements only to discard a rotten or desiccated bunch.

Marielle had her own rhythm, but she was distracted from it by her anxiety and curiosity. Watching Tomas, observing not only his skill but also his clearly practiced eye, relieved her concern that he'd be an impediment to the harvest. But she couldn't shake her unease at the fact that he was here at all.

The other members of the crew had begun a low, guttural song that rumbled up and down the row. Occasionally Janosch, transporting a full bucket of grapes, would bark an order or point out a missed cluster. Tomas continued silently, filling his basket systematically and only gesturing with his hand when he was ready for it to be emptied. He talked to no one; he did not pick up the song; and he ignored Marielle's gaze, burying himself in the task with an intensity that hovered between concentration and anger.

By ten o'clock, the morning sun had finally burned through the fog and Anita arrived with an urn of hot coffee and ham sandwiches. The crew got to their feet and stretched. A few shrugged off jackets and sweaters as the combination of vigorous labor and the heat from the sun began to warm them.

Marielle pulled off her gloves and helped her mother pass out steaming mugs of coffee and the hearty whole-grain bread their neighbor Ute Meyer sold every morning in her bakery. Marielle watched and listened as the crew took their mugs and murmured "thank you." Tomas approached and clasped the thick pottery handle Marielle held out to him, taking it from her with a nod, but barely glancing at her before he turned away.

While the others clustered in small groups, sipping their coffee and munching on their sandwiches with gusto, Tomas walked to the hillside and sat on an over-turned bucket. He resented the circumstances that forced him to be here, and he was irritated by Marielle's undisguised oversight and distrust of his work. Janosch joined him for a few minutes, leaving an animated discussion with the older men of the crew. He placed his hand on Tomas's shoulder and invited him to join the conversation. But Tomas shrugged and shook his head in refusal.

Marielle heard a sharpness in Janosch's voice but didn't understand Polish. Janosch seemed frustrated with his nephew's withdrawal but didn't waste any more words with him and returned to the group.

Anita had observed the scene, too.

"Is that one going to be a problem?"

"So far he's been surprisingly efficient. Certainly not sociable, but you've always told me we're not here for a tea party. As long as he continues working the way he did this morning, he can drink his coffee in peace wherever he wants."

"I don't recognize him—Janosch has never brought him before."

"He's Janosch's nephew. He must have worked other harvests before. He definitely knows what he's doing. I can't complain, although I find him perplexing."

"If you have any concerns about him, speak to Janosch. Don't let anything go unremarked. I've got to get back to Papa. I'll send Ute's son up around 1:30 p.m. with dinner. The weather's supposed to hold for a few more days, so get as much out of them as you can now."

She put the empty mugs in a basin and climbed into the car, leaving Marielle to call the crew back to the vines for three more hours.

For this round, she left Tomas Marek to his own labors and took up the task of collecting the contents of the buckets from each of the crew. She slipped the straps of a large open canvas knapsack over her shoulders and started at the top of the hillside, working her way down the path between rows of vines, stooping as each man dumped his bucket into her sack. Despite her bankerly life, Marielle had retained the athletic vigor of her student days, when she'd been both a long-distance runner and a rower on her university's four-women boat. During her childhood, Max had been a member of the Rheingau's kayak club and he'd taught her to manage a single kayak on the rapidly moving Rhine. Marielle's training and experience had served her and her team well, and she'd led them to a German and then a European championship.

Marielle felt the weight of the grapes on her back and straightened to her full height as she moved down the hill to the wagon with its wide plastic bin. She wanted to demonstrate to the men her ease and familiarity with the work, her strength and stamina. She was used to walking into a boardroom as the only woman and had learned how to be heard, how to be visible to those who would otherwise dismiss her. She was determined to be as much of a presence here in the vineyard.

At the end of the day, Marielle reversed her trip of the morning, returning the crew to the campgrounds after a brief trip to the grocery store so they could pick up provisions for their evening meal. Again, Tomas Marek was silent and reclusive, not joining in the banter and the give-and-take of the other crew members. On the drive back, Marielle glanced in the rearview mirror and saw him in an unguarded moment—eyes closed, skin sallow, weariness and worry etched on his face.

She said good-night and arranged the pickup time for the next morning with Janosch. Tomas had already closed the door of the camper and lit a lantern as she pulled out of the clearing.

That night, soaking in a hot tub, she felt she could enumerate each muscle in her back, her thighs and her calves. She stretched her fingers in front of her and saw not the smooth, carefully manicured hands that only last week had been tapping away on a calculator. Instead, she saw chipped nails and scratches and felt as if she were coated in a sticky layer of grape juice.

She leaned back in the tub to soak her long hair, then slid momentarily under the warm water, obliterating briefly the images and anxieties of the day.

When she emerged from the bath, muffled in an old sweatshirt and pants she'd found in the bottom of her dresser, Anita was waiting with a cup of hot cocoa and a stack of papers.

"How did it go?" She looked straight into Marielle's exhausted eyes.

Marielle nodded. "I got through the day with a decent volume. But I should go down to the tanks and check that Dieter got it all loaded…."

She set down the mug and started for the stairs.

"It's fine. Papa was already asleep, so I went down while you were in the tub."

Marielle smiled gratefully at her mother.

"How did you manage to do everything that needs to be done when you were also raising me?"

"I wasn't alone, Marielle."

CHAPTER THREE

OVER THE NEXT WEEK, the days repeated themselves in a pattern that was as familiar to her as the ancient, meter-thick walls of the winery's courtyard. The too-early alarm clock; the mug of coffee waiting in her mother's outstretched hand; the dense fog hiding the contours of the landscape in the early morning; the groggy and increasingly weary crew stamping their feet in the damp clearing of the campground waiting for their ride. The morning harvest, halting and somber as fingers stiff from the previous day and cold from the near-freezing temperatures clutched at equally cold grapes. The sun eventually burning through the grayness and giving both definition and warmth to the afternoon. The loaded wagon at sunset trundling the harvest down the hill to the tanks. And throughout it all, Tomas Marek's silence.

The rhythm of the days was familiar to Marielle because she'd spent every October of her life from childhood in these hills. She'd missed the last two years while she was in Hong Kong, but she hadn't forgotten or lost the knack of progressing along a row of vines, cradling, clipping and dropping grapes into a bucket in one swift, uninterrupted movement. The days were not a challenge to her, especially as the crew got comfortable with her expectations. They treated her with respect, thanks to Janosch.

It was the nights that filled her with anxiety. After returning the crew to the campground every evening and then grabbing some bread and cheese at her mother's insistence, she no longer soaked away the chill and aches of the day in her tub.

She headed instead to the fermentation tanks and her notebooks. She listened to the weather reports, calculated how much was in, how much was still on the vine, and worried about how much time she still had and how high the sugar content of the grapes was from each field.

She stayed late in the tiny office adjacent to the tanks, protecting herself from the cold seeping up from the concrete floor through her feet, up her cramped legs and into her spine by wrapping herself in one of Max's old coats and nursing a fiery glass of Weinbrand—the limited edition brandy Max had made every other year. She'd driven to the wine school in Geisenheim the week before the harvest began and bought a couple of textbooks on viticulture. It was during these evenings alone that she delved into the books, making notations, trying to absorb what she needed in the only way she knew how—through book learning. Marielle had always been a good student, and she tackled the harvest as if she were preparing for an exam.

But the answers eluded her, as she observed her own grapes not reacting in textbook ways.

One morning as she handed Marielle her coffee, Anita rminded her that she needed to get more rest.

"I saw the light on in the courtyard office at midnight last night. You're still as stubborn as you were as a child when you couldn't fall asleep until you'd gotten the last piece of a jigsaw puzzle to fit. Marielle, wine-making isn't a puzzle, or even an equation. Sometimes you simply aren't going to be able to solve it."

On the first Sunday of the harvest, Marielle hiked alone up to the eastern fields early in the morning to make an assessment of how much was left on the vine. The weather service was predicting an early frost later in the month. Although Max had always reserved a small vineyard close to the house for ice wine—made from grapes picked early in the day, frozen from the first frost—Marielle knew there was still too much hanging to risk harvesting it all as ice wine. She walked up and down the rows, inspecting clusters for mold or, on the contrary, underripeness. It would do no good to rush the harvest of grapes that weren't ready.

Her head ached from lack of sleep and too many glasses of Weinbrand. With a start, she realized she'd promised her mother that she would accompany her to church that morning. She hadn't been to Mass in years, and Anita herself had not been one to spend much time in the church. But since Max's illness she seemed to have found some peace in the old rituals.

Marielle jogged down the hill, slipped off her boots

in the anteroom and ran upstairs to change as her mother emerged from the bedroom.

"You're coming after all?"

"I'll be ready in ten minutes. Who's staying with Papa?"

"Bruno's downstairs in the yard fixing the axle on the wagon. He'll check on Papa for me while we're in church. He does that every Sunday."

Marielle quickly washed up, ran a comb through her long hair and put on the navy-blue suit she'd worn on the train from Frankfurt when she'd arrived the week before. It already felt stiff and unfamiliar.

Her mother was waiting in the vestibule, handbag over her wrist. They walked arm in arm down the main street of the village to St. Margarete's, two blocks away, as the bell tolled to announce the next Mass.

Marielle's eyes adjusted to the dimness inside the thick-walled medieval building that had been reconstructed since the bombing of World War II. She hurried up the aisle with Anita and knelt beside her as the priest approached the altar. Remembering the prayers, she followed along, echoing the responses out of respect for her mother, but she felt a great distance between herself and what was unfolding before her. During the sermon her mind and her glance wandered, as she observed the mostly older congregants listening intently to the priest's droning.

Her gaze stopped abruptly, however, when she recognized a man off to the side by the Madonna's altar. Tomas Marek wasn't listening to the priest, but stood in the shadows, arms folded across his chest, his face illuminated by the flickering light of the candles.

Before Mass was over, Marielle saw him light a candle and then slip out of the church through the side door. He was the last member of the Polish crew she would've expected to see in church, and, in fact, she saw three or four others in the back as she and Anita left. She nodded in greeting to them and they tipped their caps. Later in the afternoon, Marielle went back up to the vineyard—not to worry over the crop but to spend an hour sketching. It was her form of escape, to capture with a few strokes of oil pastels the broad sweep of the valley or the detail of a columbine blossom.

That evening, after checking on the tanks and the weather report, Marielle left the winery before eight, intending to finally get some rest before the week began and the push to finish the harvest intensified.

As she entered the house she thought she heard a sound that had been an indelible part of her childhood. Max at the piano. He was—had been—an accomplished musician and had given up a professional career to marry Anita and save the winery after the war. But he'd never given up the piano, at least not until his stroke, and had entertained guests throughout the season when the courtyard was open every weekend for wine tastings and festivals.

Marielle was stunned and perplexed by the music drifting down the stairs from her parents' living quarters above the public rooms of the winery. Perhaps Max had made a recording when Marielle was away. That was the only answer she could imagine as she climbed the stairs. As she got closer, she realized that what she was hearing was the piano itself, not a recording, and for an instant she felt like a child again, wishing that the music she heard meant her father had been restored to her.

When she reached the landing she slipped quietly into the living room, opposite the piano. What she saw was more surprising than if it had been the fulfillment of her wish. Max was indeed sitting in the room in his wheelchair, near but not at the piano. His eyes were closed and his hands lay still in his lap. At the piano, his back to Marielle, was Tomas Marek. His long frame was folded over the keyboard, his head bent into the music.

He improvised as spontaneously as Marielle remembered Max doing on summer evenings, at times plaintive, and then exuberant. Max, whose hearing was still acute although he could no longer speak, nodded his head, a smile of childlike joy on his face.

Rather than interrupt, Marielle hung back and retreated to the hallway, listening for a few minutes before retracing her steps down the stairs. Reaching into her pocket, she retrieved the ring that held all the keys for the winery and opened the heavy door that led to the business office where Anita kept the files.

Despite her new role in the business and her right to be in the office, Marielle had not yet abandoned the feeling that she was an interloper—an imposter pretending to be Anita who would soon be revealed as a fake.

She tried to convince herself that her concern was legitimate, but she knew she was riffling through the papers not for a management reason but a personal one.

She wanted to know who Tomas Marek was and why he was here.

In a folder in the middle drawer of the desk she found what she was looking for—copies of the visa applications that Anita had had to file with the government in order to bring the crew to the West. Marielle flipped through the alphabetically arranged pages and found "Marek, Tomas." Amid the stamps and signatures she sought the lines requiring his background. What she read stunned her. Tomas was a surgeon, educated at Jagiellonian University Medical College in Krakow, on leave from the Centralny Szpital Kliniczny (Central Clinical Hospital).

Marielle replaced the papers and returned the folder to the drawer. The music above her had stopped and she heard voices—Anita's in thanks, Tomas's mumbled response, Janosch's more voluble and emphatic conversation.

When she heard their footsteps on the stairs, she remained in the office. She could not explain her discomfort and chose to attribute her reluctance to greet them to her fatigue. Once the outer door closed behind them and Anita had coaxed Max to bed, Marielle left the office, locked the door behind her and went to bed herself.

CHAPTER FOUR

THE NEXT MORNING, still driven by the curiosity that had sent her to Anita's files, Marielle took up a position opposite Tomas on the steep Steinmorgen vineyard. Like all the mornings before this one, a damp chill pervaded the hillside and only the rustle of leaves being parted and the snap of metal clippers separating stems from vines penetrated the stillness. That morning, not even Janosch was humming.

"Your skill is exceptional," she told him. "I haven't often seen anyone except my father handle the grapes as well as you do."

Tomas nodded through the tangle of the leaves to acknowledge that she had spoken to him.

"How did you learn? Have you been at the harvest before?"

"I came as a teenager with my uncle a few times. But we worked for von Hausen then. Later, when Janosch began working for your father, I didn't come anymore."

"Why not?"

"I was studying."

"At medical school?"

Again Tomas nodded, but didn't offer more.

Marielle could see that she was falling behind in filling her bucket and resumed her silence, despite wanting to know what had brought Tomas back to the harvest. She doubted, even if she asked outright, that he would tell her.

Later, when Anita brought a cauldron of lentil soup with ham for the midday meal, she spoke briefly with Marielle.

"Last night when Janosch visited with Papa, I asked him for a favor—to work with you this evening on some of the questions I know you need answered. He's agreed to help."

Marielle started to protest, but she went on.

"Janosch has the same instincts as Papa. You're not going to find what you're looking for in textbooks. I've seen you night after night, hunched over the desk in the outer office, filling your notebook with numbers. That's only part of what you need to learn. Let Janosch help you. Don't be stubborn. You don't have that luxury. *We* don't have that luxury."

Marielle acquiesced, but only because she didn't have any other solution to the knot that had been tightening in her stomach with each passing day. Her fears for the success of the year's vintage grew more intense, especially after all the frustrating nights of trying to grasp what she needed and having the answers elude her. She was reluctant to admit her weakness to the one individual—Janosch—whose respect was vital to the completion of the harvest.

If Janosch thought she was incompetent, his opinion might spill over to the others and she'd lose control. Considering Anita's advice about establishing herself as the leader, Marielle questioned why her mother would expose her vulnerability.

She helped Anita repack the station wagon with the remains of the meal and turned back to the grapes for the rest of the afternoon without speaking to Janosch, whose eyes she avoided as she vigorously attacked a row. She worked for an hour before hoisting a collection bag on her shoulders and taking the measure of each crew member's performance as she gathered what they'd harvested since the meal. At least she could manage and even master the physical part of the harvest, she thought to herself, if not the critical decisions she knew she had to make over the next few weeks.

At the end of the day, Anita had arranged for a neighbor to drive the crew back to the campground so Janosch could stay to advise Marielle. In the small public dining room that the winery used for tastings and light meals over the winter, Anita had left a supper of bread, cold cuts and cheese and a bottle of the previous year's vintage.

Marielle went to the outer office to get her notebooks before joining Janosch in the dining room. When she returned she was surprised to see Tomas with his uncle. Her already tenuous hold on authority was disintegrating before her eyes if both Janosch and Tomas were aware of her ignorance.

She slid ungraciously into her chair, barely greeting the two men.

Janosch gestured to his nephew and spoke in halting German. "To translate, I ask him to come."

Marielle was impatient to begin and be done, desperate for the help but angry that she needed it.

The men shifted on their feet, awaiting some signal from Marielle. It finally dawned on her that they were as tired and hungry as she was and she pointed to the food.

"Please sit and eat, then we can work."

Marielle could barely swallow and took only small bites of her bread and goat cheese while Tomas and Janosch filled their plates and savored each mouthful of the simple meal. Marielle remembered her role as host and uncorked the wine, pouring three glasses. The bottle was from the Steinmorgen acreage, the same fields they'd picked that day.

Marielle knew that without looking at the label. Max had taught her that each of their patchwork of fields— both contiguous as well as scattered and each with its own name—produced distinctively flavored wines. All their grapes were Riesling, but the composition and acidity of the soil, the drainage, the angle of the sun all affected the quality and taste of the different wines. She remembered what a discovery it had been to her, to the child she was then, and how Max had made a game of it, masking the labels and having her guess with her nose whether she was tasting a Marcobrunn or a Steinmorgen or a Johannisberg. She'd loved to accompany him on the Feast of the Ascension, when he'd led a group of guests on a hike throughout their vineyards. At each field a trestle table had been set up with wine made from the grapes grown in that soil the previous year. At the end of the hike, at the top of the northernmost field, Anita was waiting with vintner's stew and cucumber salad and crusty bread to soak up the sauce. Often there'd been forty or fifty guests, sunburned, sated, enjoying the view of the valley as they sat at the outdoor feast.

Marielle said a silent prayer to the memory of those days and hoped she'd have the wines to serve next spring when she would lead the hike herself for the first time.

Reminded of why she was sitting here with Janosch, she opened her notebook as he wiped the crumbs from his lips.

"Shall we begin?" she said, reining in her anxiety.

For the next two hours, Janosch spoke to her through Tomas, trying to convey in words what he sensed through his fingertips and his nose. He tried to articulate what for him was as instinctive as breathing. Marielle kept seeking specifics—measurements, temperature, chemical analysis. But Janosch had no notebooks, no records like a chemist in a lab. He tapped his head and his heart.

"It's all in here. I watched and learned from my father. He taught me how to recognize when the grapes are ready to be picked, when the fermentation has reached its optimum.

"Max knew these things. If you'd been at his side

you would know them, as well, instead of searching in the pages of a book."

Marielle felt her face redden, her humiliation intensified by Tomas's presence. Although she'd followed her father around as a little girl, she'd abandoned his side once her studies began. From the time she was fourteen she'd propelled herself through school, preparing for the university qualifying exam—the *Abitur*—long before her classmates had begun to apply themselves to learning. When Desiree Schultz, the daughter of a neighboring vintner, had been elected queen of the wine festival the year she and Marielle were eighteen, Marielle had ignored the entire event in order to study. Hadn't that paid off for her? She'd won a place in economics at a prestigious university, graduated with honors, been hired immediately by Deutsche Bank, the only woman to secure such a position.

To prove herself in that environment, Marielle had continued to do what she knew best. She worked long hours at her desk, running regression analyses, poring over columns of numbers and pages of graphs, always prepared at meetings where she was the only woman at the table. She'd been relentless with herself in learning as much as she could and had earned respect for her diligence and intelligence. It hadn't been easy, but it had been familiar territory, concepts she knew she could grasp. The challenge of proving herself to a phalanx of skeptical men in suits had not been fraught with terror, as the task before her now was.

She looked at the two men sitting across from her

at a table whose scratches and patina she knew intimately. Their drab and ill-fitting Eastern European clothing, their slumped and weary postures and unshaven faces were a sharp contrast to the bankers in their tailored suits. But Marielle was intimidated by these men, resistant to what Janosch was trying to teach her and frustrated that he couldn't articulate what she needed in a way she could understand. It wasn't merely the gulf between his Polish and her German, but the distance between a man of the earth and a woman of the mind.

At ten in the evening, the second bottle of wine emptied, Marielle closed her notebook, finally giving in to everyone's fatigue and the knowledge that the next day would be upon them far too soon. She offered to drive the men to the campground but Tomas told her Anita had offered them two old bikes that had been sitting unused in the shed. They would pedal back.

When they left, Marielle cleared the plates and washed up in the winery's café kitchen; the sound of running water hid her tears.

The next morning in the vineyard, Tomas approached her during the break. She was startled to have him initiate a conversation with her. She saw the dark circles under his eyes and regretted how long she'd kept him the night before.

"I'm sorry for the late hour yesterday evening. I'm sure when Janosch said yes to my mother he didn't realize how much help I needed."

"It's not the time that my uncle regretted as much as

his inability to teach you. Or rather, in his words, your inability to learn."

The briefest smile skimmed across Tomas's face, the first time Marielle had seen any emotion at all. She was stung by Janosch's criticism but felt that Tomas was attempting to make light of it.

"He's an old man, set in his ways, who has little use for the science of winemaking. He believes that too much science will destroy the unique character of each wine—create a dull uniformity that relies on duplicating a formula over and over instead of experimenting and trusting one's instincts."

"And what do you believe?"

"I'm somewhere in the middle. I have great respect for my uncle and I understand his frustration with the factory mentality of the Party's approach to winemaking in Poland. But I *am* a scientist. In the same way that I rely upon both my training and my instincts when I encounter a problem during surgery, I believe one needs both to produce a successful vintage."

"So you disagree with your uncle?"

"To a certain extent. For example, I don't think you're unteachable." Again, the flicker of a smile.

"It sounds as if Janosch has given up on me."

"But I haven't. I have an offer to make you. I know enough about the science and the art of winemaking that I think I can show you what you need to learn. Will you allow me to help on my own? Not as a translator of Polish, but as a translator of the intangible?"

"Why would you?"

"Because my uncle is a friend of your father's and does not want to disappoint him. And because my uncle's reputation is his livelihood, so a failed harvest will reflect badly on him. There are many families in Poland who are dependent on Janosch's ability to bring the crew to this vineyard year after year. What we're able to earn here in one season we can't make in a whole year in Poland. Not even I, as a physician. I know you've wondered what would bring someone like me to work the harvest. You have no idea, here in the West, how little our economy can support. I'm not the only one on the crew who's an educated professional. Tadeusz is a civil engineer. Matthias is a teacher of mathematics. But they can't feed their families—I cannot feed mine—without the work in your vineyards. If you fail, many people will suffer."

Marielle stood with her arms folded across her chest listening and absorbing Tomas's message. Her burdens were increasing, as if she carried a heavily laden basket of grapes on her shoulders. She shifted her weight and straightened her back, not willing to be daunted by the magnitude of the responsibility.

"What are you proposing?" she asked.

"I'll stay behind in the evenings as we did last night and work with you. I can't promise you success, but I can give you the tools you'll need to make success possible. The rest is up to you, the weather, the market."

Marielle felt herself stiffen as her terror surfaced again—in broad daylight on the hillside instead of in the darkness and solitude of night.

Tomas saw the expression on her face and felt a brief stab of compassion for her struggle to fill her father's shoes.

"There will always be risk. Always elements you can't control. I can't give you predictability and certainty, if that's what you're looking for."

Marielle shook her head. She'd learned with Max's stroke that life was not predictable and certain. She understood intellectually that, even with as much science as she could get her hands on, she would still face obstacles. But in the past she'd been able to rely on herself, find the resources within to solve her problems. She hated having to trust someone else.

Tomas, taking her silence as a refusal, shrugged and turned away.

"Fine, suit yourself."

"Wait."

Marielle unclasped her tightly entwined arms and reached out to touch him on the shoulder. He stopped, but didn't turn around.

"I accept your offer. Please stay this evening."

He nodded brusquely. "Bring the harvest records for the last ten years. Perhaps we can identify some patterns."

And he walked away, pulling his gloves out of his pockets as he took up a position on the row where he'd left off.

That evening, after driving the rest of the crew back to the campground, Marielle prepared a platter of Parma ham, cheese and pickles and carried it out to the fermentation room where Tomas was making notations. They ate quickly and silently before spreading the records of the last decade across a worktable. Heads bent, they studied the numbers, pointing out exceptions or oddities, marginal notes about weather aberrations, anything that could give them clues to the success or failure of a vintage.

They worked till nine. Marielle would have persisted, pushed herself to stay longer, but she felt guilty about keeping Tomas late the night before and knew she had to balance her need for him now with the work that awaited them the next day.

"You should go, get some rest."

"So should you. You can't make good decisions if you're sleep-deprived."

"Yes, Doctor."

As she gathered up the paperwork and turned off the lights, Tomas pulled his bicycle from the shed. Although he was still an enigma to her, Marielle felt a sense of reassurance as she watched him pedal away toward the river. She shut the gate to the courtyard and closed the latch. Wrapping her sweater around her, she climbed the stairs to her room. Despite her agreement to get some rest, she didn't sleep right away but studied her notes. She found no answers yet, but knew she'd made a beginning.

For the remainder of the harvest she met with Tomas nearly every night, listening, absorbing, struggling to assimilate what he had to impart. One evening he asked her to characterize each of the last ten years' vintages— to describe them not with data but with words, images.

"I don't even remember some of them. I wasn't here during many of those years."

"How can you be a vintner if you don't know your own history? It's one of my frustrations with the Party in Poland—they're trying to create a new society without memory. You can't abandon responsibility for what came before simply because you were sitting at a desk in Frankfurt. That's not who you are anymore."

"These lessons are supposed to be about winemaking, not who I am or am not." Marielle spoke to him as she would have to a subordinate, not a colleague.

"Very well. If you can't remember, then I suggest we retrieve bottles from each of the vintages and start tasting."

They trudged down to the wine cellar and filled a crate with the long-necked brown bottles that were standard for the region. When the crate was full, Marielle insisted on carrying it to the dumbwaiter and hoisting the rope that sent the load to the upper level.

In silence she set out a basket of crackers and a tray full of tasting glasses etched with her mother's seal. Then she began uncorking bottles.

Her fury at being lectured by Tomas masked the fear she felt at having no definable identity. He was right that she was no longer a banker. But she had nothing to replace that role, nothing that was hers. To Janosch and the crew she was merely the daughter of the chief, not the chief herself. She assumed that Tomas also saw her as unformed, amorphous, filling the shape of whatever vessel was presented to her: the hardy field worker, shouldering as much weight as the men or the dilettante vintner, acting the role but not truly embracing it. His accusation had stung so sharply because she felt adrift, unsuited for the title of "vintner." If she wasn't a banker anymore—and she wasn't—or a vintner, who was she?

When she finished uncorking all the bottles, she started with the oldest and poured them a taste of 0.1 liter from every year and every vineyard. She picked up the first glass, looked Tomas in the eye and raised it slightly in a mock toast.

"To your experiment."

With each glass she made notations, searching for words to describe the wines. Tomas drank with her. At first, Marielle was deliberately sullen, recording her impressions only in writing and not sharing them with Tomas. To her surprise, he didn't object.

"This isn't an exam, you know. I'm not a teacher waiting for you to recite back my lectures. You're your own teacher here." And he raised his glass containing the 1969 Marcobrunn Spätlese.

Tomas's remark released some of the pressure she always felt to perform well at every task. As she proceeded into the neat rows of glasses she'd arrayed on the table, she began to make discoveries—subtle differences, echoes, textures. Max had taught her to appreciate and enjoy wine, but this evening with Tomas began to reveal a complexity and beauty that ten years' worth of data had not. It also made her drunk. Even though they took only a sip from each glass, there were nevertheless many of them. Her reserve, the way she normally presented herself, began to dissolve. At one point she exclaimed over the quality of a wine she'd just sipped and launched into a verbal description that reopened the conversation with Tomas. As she tasted and noted the year on the bottle, she pulled out of her memory anecdotes of particular experiences when she'd worked the harvest.

"The weather was so warm that year—not like now. I remember wearing a yellow T-shirt and shorts and the sweat dripping down my back.

"That was the year the Auslese won a gold medal. I came home for the dinner to congratulate my father. I was sitting next to him when one of his colleagues asked what he'd done differently and he answered that winemaking was like jazz. Improvisational. Inspired by the moment, by the energy of those around him, by the emotions within. By the willingness to shift tempo or key and head off in a new direction."

As she spoke, the memories became less about the wine and more about her relationship with Max.

"You're very close to your father, aren't you?" Tomas asked.

"Yes. Are your parents still alive? Healthy?"

"My mother is. She lives with us in Warsaw, works as a bookkeeper. My father died before I was born. My older sister, although she was only four, remembers the day my mother, who was pregnant with me, learned of his death."

"I'm sorry—for her, and for you that you never knew your father."

"Janosch has been a father to me. My mother turned to him, her brother, and he stepped in. It's because of him that I went to university and studied medicine. I was an angry boy in my teens. I wanted to be a musician."

"But you *are* a musician!"

He raised his eyebrows to question how she knew that. Marielle felt her face redden.

"You were listening the night I played for your father?"

"Sound travels in the house. I couldn't help overhearing you. You were good. And you made my father happy, for which I'm most grateful."

"So you were watching, as well."

"I didn't want to intrude. My father's face was so blissful. If I'd said anything, I would've broken your spell."

"I hope my daughter grows to love me as much as you love Max."

"Your daughter? How old is she? Is she with your wife while you're here?"

"Magdalena is seven. My wife is gone and Magdalena lives with me and my mother and our old nanny, who cared for my sister and me while my mother worked. Now she cares for Magdalena. I miss her. She doesn't understand why I'm away for so long. I worry that when I go back, she'll turn away from me for abandoning her."

"Don't worry. Speaking as a daughter, I can assure you that she'll forgive you."

The glasses were empty. The notebook was full. It was 1:00 a.m.

"I should help you wash up before I head back to the campground." He rose and began to place glasses on the tray.

"I'm concerned about you cycling back at this late hour, and I've had too much wine to drive you. Why don't you sleep here? I can make a bed for you on the couch in the office."

"No, it's too much trouble. I'll be careful."

"It's no trouble at all. If you *don't* stay, I'll worry about your safety all night. Would you start the washing up while I get the bedding?"

Marielle left before he could protest again and tiptoed up to her room to retrieve pillows and a duvet from her trunk. By the time she'd made up a bed for him, he was placing the last glass on the drying rack.

She handed him a towel and a bar of soap and pointed out the bathroom.

"I'll have a mug of coffee waiting for you in the kitchen at 5:00 a.m. Sleep well. And thank you."

Tomas watched as she turned and walked up the stairs, notebook tucked under her arm. It had been a long time since he had revealed so much of himself. He wasn't sure if it had been the wine or the vulnerable young woman whose memories had released his own.

CHAPTER FIVE

A FEW DAYS LATER, Marielle experienced a far different form of Tomas's help. A rainstorm rose quickly in the vineyard late in the afternoon, an isolated squall that came with little warning, black clouds looming over the mountains carrying a disastrous cargo of water and wind. Because their backs were turned from the mountains and the sky across the river to the south was still a luminous blue, the harvest crew didn't sense the storm until it was upon them. Huge drops of rain fell first, splattering across head and hands, shaking the broad leaves, sending the birds on the hillside into scattered flight.

Normally, rain didn't deter the pickers. Although uncomfortable, they continued on, sometimes at a slower pace as shears became slippery or visibility blurred. But Janosch, emptying a load of grapes into the wagon, saw the ominous blackness descending and yelled in warning to Marielle and the rest of the crew. A bolt of lightning arced down into the trees above them. He threw a canvas tarp over the wagon and secured it with rope just as the deluge began.

Marielle called the others away from the vines and most of them withdrew to huddle under the long flaps of the canvas. Tadeusz, on the eastern side of the row, motioned that he'd finish his side, with only a few meters to go. Marielle nodded an okay.

She watched in dismay as the rain pelted the fragile fruit, unsure how much of it would withstand the downpour. The rain was so heavy that it had already cut into the aisles between the vines, forming streams of mud and stones that poured down the hillside.

Suddenly, a swath of churning water came rushing toward them from above, bringing with it the debris of the hillside to the north—broken vines, rocks the size of a man's head, a pair of rusted and forgotten shears, a glove.

"The creek that runs across the field must have overrun its banks," Janosch shouted to her over the din of the hammering rain.

Their location huddled around the wagon placed them just beyond the reach of the rising water that was gathering momentum as it raced down the hillside. Except for Tadeusz, who couldn't hear their shouts and didn't see the water until it was at his knees.

The others watched in horror as the water lifted him, carrying him away as if he were a leaf and not a 150-pound man. He grabbed hold of a branch but the force of the water was so strong that it ripped the whole vine out of the earth with its root intact and swept them both farther down the hillside. Marielle saw the fear in Tadeusz's eyes as the water turned him on his back and he disappeared over the next drop in the hill.

Tomas and Matthias bolted from the shelter of the wagon, parallel to the destructive channel formed by the roiling water. They found Tadeusz unconscious, his body halted by an outcropping of rock. They managed to pull him away from the rising water to soggy but safer ground. Marielle, her fears for her grapes now replaced by concern for Tadeusz, ran to meet them.

Tomas was bent over Tadeusz's limp body, breathing into his mouth, then beginning chest compressions. He worked silently and confidently, undeterred by the blood streaming for Tadeusz's forehead where he'd been battered by the rocks.

Marielle stood back with Matthias, sheets of rain drenching her, as Tomas continued. When he saw her, he asked her to protect Tadeusz's head from the rain. She stripped off her waterproof anorak and held it over him, keeping the water away from his face. Tomas worked tirelessly, his movements purposeful and focused, alternating between compressions and breathing.

Finally, Tadeusz coughed, his chest heaving, and Tomas rolled him onto his side as muddy water was expelled from his mouth. With Tadeusz breathing on his own, Tomas carefully checked him for bruises. It was then that he and Marielle saw the oddly twisted orientation of his left leg.

"The impact of being thrown against the rock must have broken it," he said. He shouted to Matthias, "Can you find me something to use as a splint?"

Matthias returned with a discarded post that looked

long enough and strong enough for Tomas's purpose. Marielle took the cotton scarf from around her neck and tore it into strips. At Tomas's direction, she held Tadeusz's head in her lap.

"Hold him down if you can. This is going to be excruciatingly painful for him."

With deft, sure hands, Tomas aligned the broken leg and bound it to the splint.

"That should prevent further damage until we can get him off the hillside."

The rain continued unabated. Marielle was reluctant to risk another life by sending someone down to lower ground to obtain help and decided to wait out the storm. From her vantage point, she could see that the village square had been flooded by the overflowing creek. Flashes from fire engines and rescue vehicles indicated that the danger and destruction had not been confined to the vineyards.

Marielle and Tomas were soaked to the skin. Tomas had removed his coat to cover Tadeusz to conserve his body temperature. He held Tadeusz's hand, occasionally checking his pulse, and spoke to him in calming tones. Marielle stroked his head, which she still supported in her lap. Although the color had drained from his face and it was creased in pain, he was conscious and breathing.

Tomas looked across at Marielle and nodded.

"Thank you," he said.

"Thank *you*. You saved his life."

As the rain finally subsided, Marielle saw headlights

climbing the hill and realized with relief that it was
Anita in the station wagon. She brought with her the
news that two people had drowned, trapped in a
basement apartment. A pregnant woman and her little
girl had been swept through the village in their Volkswagen, but had managed to escape when the car
collided with a streetlight in the square.

After Anita's arrival, they improvised a stretcher and
carried Tadeusz to the car. Tomas rode with him to the
hospital in Eltville, and Marielle turned to her rain-
soaked, debris-strewn land. She sent the crew down
with the wagon to the winery when she could see that
the water below had receded, but stayed on the hillside
by herself to assess how much she'd lost.

She trekked across the fields, counting up the
damaged rows, holding back her fear. The destruction
was limited to the single field where they'd been
working that afternoon, a result of the path taken by the
unleashed creek. Although the crew would need to
spend a day or two at the end of the harvest in clean up,
most of the grapes still on the vine had been spared. She
was grateful for that, but more grateful for the life
spared that afternoon and for Tomas's presence on the
hillside—and in her life.

CHAPTER SIX

AFTER THE STORM, Marielle's confidence grew as she tackled the remaining days of the harvest. The yield promised to be higher than she'd anticipated. The weather held, and only the small acreage near the house was left when the first frost settled on the valley. The crew had the vines picked clean by the time the sun began to warm the earth—perfect conditions for ice wine. Although she still had much ahead of her before the success of the vintage would be apparent, Marielle no longer felt out of control or terrorized by what she didn't know.

The morning of November 11 dawned crisp and clear. It was *Martinstag,* the feast of St. Martin. The winery planned to open its doors that evening for a small celebration after the traditional parade and bonfire in the village. Around four in the afternoon, just before sunset, Joseph Krechel, one of the tallest men in the village and a fireman, donned the costume of a Roman centurion, complete with plumed helmet, polished breastplate and red cape. He mounted Hans

Schmid's white stallion, whose bridle was decorated as lavishly as Joseph himself, and horse and rider arrived in the square in front of the church. A hundred children from the kindergarten and the elementary school waited impatiently with their parents, lanterns hanging from long sticks swinging restlessly in their small hands. As soon as Joseph took his place at the head of the line, the firemen's band brought their horns to their lips and began to play. Parents lit the lanterns and the procession moved forward, the horse prancing and the children singing about the unselfish St. Martin, who cut his cloak into two pieces and gave one to a freezing beggar.

All along the route of the procession, townspeople watched, some joining in the singing and walking with the children. By darkness they'd come to an open field at the edge of the village, where the fire brigade had built a towering pile of scrap wood and roped it off. The children formed a circle around the wood. Joseph dismounted, removed his red cloak and draped it over Gregor Sperling, who'd played the beggar with great gusto every year since he'd graduated from high school. Then Joseph took a torch from a waiting colleague and lit the wood.

To the excitement of the children, the fire rose quickly through the towering pile. Ute Meyer began moving around the outer circle, distributing her large, doughy pretzels encrusted with salt crystals.

Marielle had not attended the St. Martin's Fire since she'd left the village. It wasn't a tradition that adapted well to a dense urban environment like Frankfurt. She had walked down to the field with the procession when it passed by the winery and she stood now, pulling apart one of Ute's pretzels as the flames crackled and shot into the air.

Tomas had been leaving Gruber's Appliance Store where he'd spent some of his harvest earnings on a toaster and a Bosch coffeemaker for his mother. He saw the bobbing lanterns of the children turn the corner at the end of the square and felt a pang for Magdalena. She'd made a lantern for today, as well, decorated with leaf rubbings, his mother had written him in her last letter. He decided to follow the procession for a short distance, sharing in his daughter's experience a thousand kilometers away.

When he got to the bonfire he saw Marielle across the clearing and watched her face in the firelight. He saw both exhaustion and tenacity reflected in her expression. Her hair fell in loose waves around her shoulders instead of in the severe braid she'd worn throughout the harvest. He had considered her attractive before, but in a conventional way. Tonight, however, watching her in an unguarded moment, singing with the children, he was touched by her vulnerability and openness. She looked beautiful to him. An unexpected wave of tenderness washed over him as he stood on the periphery of the circle. Her circle. Her life. Not his, he reminded himself, and turned away with his shopping bags.

The next morning, their campers stowed with Miele washing machines and other West German goods purchased with some of the Deutschmarks they'd earned, the Polish crew got ready to depart from the campground. As Tomas and Janosch made final preparations, Marielle pulled into the clearing and jumped out of the car. She had two packages in her arms and breathlessly approached the two men.

"I was worried that you'd already left," she murmured. "I had these for you last night, but you didn't come by." She tried not to sound plaintive, but her voice was tinged with disappointment and internally she winced at her own neediness.

"I wanted to say thank you, to both of you."

She handed Janosch the larger bundle. "My mother told me of your fondness for hazelnuts. I hope you enjoy this."

To Tomas she held out a flat package about the size of a book.

"On Sundays I did some painting. I've noticed how you look out over the valley during breaks and I thought you might like this small memento."

Tomas unwrapped the package and held up a watercolor of the scene that had surrounded him for the last six weeks.

"Thank you." He took Marielle's hand and shook it. "Goodbye. My best wishes to your parents."

Marielle stood in the middle of the campground as the crew formed a caravan and headed out onto the highway. She stared after the gray ribbon of ancient vehicles until it was out of sight.

CHAPTER SEVEN

ON JANUARY 5 Max died in his sleep. He had enjoyed the Christmas holidays with Anita and Marielle and watched the fireworks on New Year's Eve from the upstairs parlor windows that looked out over the river. It had been too cold to take him to the top of the hillside where he and Marielle had always watched when she was a girl.

Anita came to wake Marielle. She was still in her robe and slippers and Marielle knew immediately that something had happened. It was unlike Anita not to be dressed for the day well before Marielle ventured from her bed.

"What's wrong?" she asked her mother as Anita gently called her name.

"Papa is gone." And she took Marielle in her arms.

After the funeral Marielle helped Anita sort and answer the condolences that had flooded into the winery as news of Max's death had spread. In the stack of envelopes that had not yet been opened she found one with a Polish stamp addressed to her. She reacted with a sharp physical pain in her chest, as if she'd been startled by a loud noise in the middle of the night. She put the envelope aside to open later in the privacy of her room.

The paper was a thin, cheaply made sheet the color of dirty dishwater and the words had been formed with a ballpoint pen that skipped occasionally. But as she read the words she saw Tomas's long fingers moving across the page and heard his voice as if they were sitting in the winery late at night. His letter was tender and thoughtful, remembering how much Marielle had loved Max and calling to mind the images she'd described the night she drank too much.

"You hold much of your father within yourself. Don't forget that as you mourn him, because he lives on in you. He was a fortunate man to have a daughter like you, Marielle, and I know he loved you."

For the first time since the morning of Max's death, Marielle cried, trying not to spill her tears on the fragile paper for fear it would disintegrate. That Tomas understood her loss and the special nature of her connection to her father touched her deeply. His empathy spoke to what Marielle believed must be his relationship to his own daughter. But it took her breath away that he understood the guilt she felt in not being the natural vintner Max had been. Throughout the fall she'd berated herself for not paying more attention when she was younger, for not being present for so much of her adult life. When she'd left home for university and the wider world, she wondered if Max had ever regretted her going or felt that she'd turned her back on him. She wondered if Max had even been aware that she'd taken on his responsibilities in those last months.

As these thoughts overwhelmed her, her body was engulfed in sobs—both for her father and for the man in Warsaw who was offering her hope and forgiveness.

The next morning she woke at dawn to Tomas's letter on her night table and sat at her desk, still wearing her nightgown, to answer him. She expressed her gratitude for his understanding and for the kindness he'd shown Max during the harvest. She reminded him of the joy she'd seen on Max's face the night Tomas played the piano for him. She didn't trust herself to write about the depth of her own feelings when she'd read Tomas's note. She didn't reveal how deeply he'd touched her and how much he'd seen into her soul.

Later that morning she added her letter to the stack of acknowledgments she'd written for Anita and took them to the post office. And then she waited, not conscious that she was keeping track of the days it would take for the post to reach Warsaw, be delivered and read by Tomas, allow him to respond and then for the response to travel back to her. That she was waiting for a reply seemed foolish to her—ridiculous to want something so unattainable. He'd probably written merely out of courtesy and by accident had found the words that spoke so directly to her. He had no intention, she was sure, of continuing the correspondence. When two weeks had passed without a reply, she acknowledged that her expectations had indeed been unrealistic, and she was relieved that she'd been restrained in her reply to him.

She tried to put him out of her mind.

She threw herself into the winter rhythm of the winery—preparations for the bottling of the harvest, calls to customers confirming their orders, plans to schedule the concerts and performances that took place every summer in the courtyard, equipment maintenance that needed to be done. She was in the office on the morning of February 14 when she heard the doorbell. Anita had gone to do the marketing so Marielle answered the door. Maria Marangoudakis, a Greek immigrant who ran the florist shop in the railroad station, stood on the stoop with an elaborately wrapped bouquet.

"It's for you, Marielle—not a late funeral arrangement. The request came by wire from Warsaw."

She handed over the flowers with a twinkle in her eye and climbed back onto her bicycle. The attached cart was filled with more flowers destined for others in the village who would soon be smiling as broadly as Marielle.

Marielle took the bouquet into the winery kitchen to find a vase large enough for the dozen long-stemmed roses that she discovered under the layers of cellophane and yards of ribbon. The roses were a deep burgundy with petals like velvet. Tucked deep inside the center of the bouquet was an envelope with her name on it, scrawled in Maria's hand. But inside the envelope was the printed copy of the wire itself, with the order for the roses and the text of the message. Her hand trembled as she unfolded the yellow sheet of paper and read what it held.

Dear Marielle,

Happy Valentine's Day! Although such frivolities are discouraged, I thought that a gift of flowers for you alone (and not simply in memory of your dear father) would be a way to brighten what has been a dark winter for you. Your note reminded me of the many hours I spent at your side during the harvest and how much I miss your curiosity and drive and tenacity. I have framed the painting you gave me and it hangs in my office at the clinic—a constant reminder of the woman who painted it and what she sees every day. It links me to you. Forgive me if the roses are inappropriate—a gift that should come from a lover rather than a friend. I thought of making up some excuse about florists only having roses today, but the truth is, I asked for roses.

Yours,
Tomas

Marielle read the note over and over, her eyes leaping from one phrase to the next. Were these the words of a friend, or of a man who wished to be more than a friend? Why had he chosen Valentine's Day to send the flowers if he only intended a gesture of friendship? Why was she feeling such turmoil? She wanted with all her heart to simply enjoy the lush and lavish burst of color and not agonize over its meaning. She was shocked by how quickly her perception of Tomas had changed when he'd written her after Max's death and understood her so clearly. Had she been denying her own feelings toward him? Had those feelings only been allowed to blossom after he'd left and was no longer a man she employed—a man who was a thousand kilometers away? Marielle didn't know what to do with her feelings.

She brought the vase into the office and placed it on her desk, where its emphatic presence filled her sight and she could inhale its rich scent.

When Anita returned she stopped in the office and saw the bouquet.

"Who are these from?"

"Tomas Marek."

Anita looked at Marielle with curiosity.

Marielle shrugged. She wasn't ready to admit her wonder at what was happening between her and Tomas.

"A belated condolence," she explained. "I'll send him a thank-you note."

That evening, Marielle struggled with her response. She was surprised by her longing for Tomas, a longing that had been muffled through the winter by the strain of Max's deteriorating condition and death. She'd been so preoccupied with the impending loss of her father that she hadn't recognized her sense of loss after Tomas's departure. She'd been lonely during the winter, but she'd thought it was because she'd left friends and colleagues behind in Frankfurt. Her life, now dictated by the demands of the land, the seasons, no longer intersected with lives driven by urban commerce. Even though Frankfurt was only fifty kilometers from the

Rheingau, it had become increasingly rare for her friends to visit. Evenings spent laughing over a glass of wine as a release from the pressures of business were no longer a part of her life. But she realized she didn't miss those evenings at all. She realized that what she missed were Tomas Marek's hands—gesturing in the dim light of the fermentation room as he explained a concept, or cradling a cluster of grapes in the autumn sunshine, or brushing against hers as he gathered up the papers strewn across her desk.

She tried to imagine him in Warsaw, composing his note to her late in the evening after he returned home from the clinic and spent an hour reading to Magdalena before putting her to bed. She saw his hands again, gently moving a strand of Magdalena's hair away from her face as she slept, pulling the comforter up around her shoulders to ward off the chill in the poorly heated apartment. She saw his hands loving and protecting, and longed for them to love and protect her.

That longing was impossible to fulfill. It stilled her own hands, and she found she couldn't write to him at all.

The next morning she sent a brief wire assuring him the flowers had arrived, that they were beautiful and that she was deeply moved by his words and his gift. She didn't want to appear ungrateful for what had been an extraordinary expense for him. She was overwhelmed, in fact, by the extravagance of what he'd done and said. But she held in check her hope that the longing she felt was shared by him.

She spent the day impatient and irritable, thrusting

crates of empty bottles out of her way, when two days before she'd stacked them in the courtyard exactly where she'd wanted them. She broke the pen she was using to fill out some order forms when she pressed too hard, splattering ink across the page and onto her shirt. In the kitchen at midday she slammed cupboard doors and tore open a package of noodles, spilling most of them on the floor.

Anita, as if dealing with an unruly toddler, said nothing and retrieved her dustpan and whiskbroom from the closet and began sweeping up.

"I'm sorry, Mama. Let me clean up the mess."

"It's nothing, almost done. Why don't you put the water on to boil and I'll finish."

"I can't seem to do anything right today. Everything, even the slightest inconvenience, is annoying me."

"When you were younger, you used to act like this when you had to make a choice about something and were afraid."

"Afraid?"

"Afraid of taking a risk. When you were learning to walk, you couldn't quite bring yourself to let go and take a step. But it made you so angry that you'd throw your toys. You wanted so much to go, but a part of you always held back. Cautious. Tentative. Your frustration was so palpable. Like it is now."

Marielle looked at her mother.

"What's holding you back? Are you afraid he doesn't love you as much as you love him? We never truly know another's feelings. It's like the leap of faith

you had to take this fall with the vintage. Trust your instincts, even when you don't have all the data. And
believe me, any other woman who received a bouquet
like you did yesterday would consider that all the data
she needed."

"How did you know?"

"I knew before he left here in November. You may
not have recognized it in yourselves, but when the two
of you were together you radiated. I saw him watching
you when you weren't aware of it. He couldn't take his
eyes off you."

"It's hopeless, of course. That's why I'm so paralyzed.
He's in Warsaw. I'm here. If I let myself love him—open
the Pandora's Box of my emotions—we're only setting
ourselves up for heartache and disappointment."

"If you ask me, the Pandora's Box has already been
opened, and if you try to stuff your feelings back in,
you'll just face more days like today filled with anger
and frustration.

"Your father and I were separated for years during
the war. Months went by with no word from him. But
our love survived. You'll find a way."

"What should I do?"

"I can't tell you that, Marielle. But you'll know. Be
still and listen—to yourself and to him."

The next day, her answer came in the form of another
wire from Tomas.

"Come to Warsaw for Easter," it said.

And she did.

CHAPTER EIGHT

April 1976

HER BAGS WERE FILLED with gifts. A doll and picture books for Magdalena; stockings and well-made gloves for Tomas's mother, Halina; handkerchiefs and a merino wool shawl for Nyanya, the nurse who had cared for Tomas as a child and now looked after Magdalena; and food for the Easter meal—ham and oranges and cheese and fresh peas. She also brought some of Anita's plum preserves and cookies that she'd baked herself the night before she left and packed between layers of waxed paper in a tin.

The train ride was long and complicated, across West Germany, into Czechoslovakia through Prague and then north into Poland. At border crossings in the middle of the night she woke to the insistent knocking of guards on her compartment door. Flashlights flicked from her papers to her face and she had the chilling sense that she could be denied entry or worse if she answered the gruff, rude questioning of the border guards incorrectly.

Exhausted, she arrived in Warsaw two days after her departure from Frankfurt. She washed her face in the lavatory with the trickle of water that was left, rebraided her hair and put on some lipstick as the train pulled into the Central Station. She made her way down the platform seeking Tomas's familiar face but seeing only strangers.

At the end of the platform she put down her bags and waited. There was a grayness to the building and to the faces surrounding her. Soldiers with Kalishnikov rifles slung over their shoulders patrolled the main concourse. In contrast to the hectic pace of the Frankfurt station, travelers moved more slowly and there were far fewer than she'd expected to see. There were one or two food stalls selling sausages and one aqua-blue cart offering orange drinks served by a kerchief-bedecked older woman. She rinsed out her glasses in a murky dishpan and then reused them, selling orange juice mixed with seltzer. A newsstand was the only other sign of commerce. There was no florist or restaurant. The space was cavernous, but remarkably empty.

She was startled when she felt a hand on her shoulder.

"I'm sorry I'm late," he murmured as she turned toward him.

She took in his gaze, his dark eyes ringed by circles of fatigue, his skin no longer showing the effects of six weeks in the open autumn air but reflecting the same gray-tinged pallor she'd seen on others in the station. She reached up to touch the face she'd been imagining for weeks as his hands encircled her shoulders and he bent to kiss her.

At first, he offered her the platonic continental greeting of a kiss on each cheek. But the proximity of their bodies, the sensation of his cheek against her skin and the memory of his scent as he leaned in toward her caused her to move closer into the circle of his arms. The tension of the long journey began to loosen and her body softened, molding itself to the contours of Tomas's angular frame.

He was thinner than she remembered as he pulled her even closer, wrapping his arms tightly around her. His lips moved from her cheek to her mouth and she felt as if he was breathing life into her, not only reviving her after the exhausting journey, but also filling her up after the emptiness and loss of the winter.

He didn't stop kissing her. After her mouth, he kissed her eyes, her neck, her fingertips. A smile lit her face and he laughed out loud.

"I can't believe you're here and in my arms."

"I can't believe it, either. I don't recognize myself right now. I feel like a madwoman or an addict."

He lifted her. She felt the strength in his arms and placed herself in his care, allowing him to carry not only her body but her spirit.

"My mother and Magdalena are waiting at the apartment. I'll have to let you go long enough for them to satisfy their curiosity."

He gathered her suitcases and led her to the street and the trolley.

She sat by the window and at his urging looked out at the city instead of at him. He held her hand, his long fingers entwined with hers, gently stroking as if to convince them both that their presence together was real, confirmed by the evidence of touch, skin, pulse.

They changed trolleys twice before arriving at his apartment block on the outskirts of the city. There was no elevator and he carried her bags up the narrow staircase to the sixth floor. Vestiges of cabbage and onion permeated the stairwell. They passed others descending the stairs and Marielle was aware of the blatant glances sweeping over her from her head to her shoes. Everything about her looks and her clothing screamed "Western economy." She had noted as she watched from the tram that even the young women were dressed drably in shapeless clothing. She'd never considered herself overly concerned with style, but her well-made skirt and sweater and especially her shoes had drawn excessive interest.

She wondered if she would be causing Tomas difficulty as so obviously a Western woman.

When they got to the landing, she stopped worrying about the impact of her clothing. She could hear the chatter of a young girl, querulous and insistent, behind one of the doors, and a much older voice answering her.

Tomas placed his key in the lock.

"Papa!"

Marielle stepped back as Magdalena leaped into his arms. She peeked over Tomas's shoulder at Marielle and stared at her, then whispered in Tomas's ear. He whirled around with Magdalena still in his arms and welcomed Marielle into the cramped hallway of the apartment. Standing at the end of the hall by the kitchen was an older woman, her head shrouded in a cotton scarf, her housedress covered with an apron, her back bent with years of physical work. She nodded at Marielle but did not smile when Tomas introduced her as Nyanya.

Magdalena continued to demand her father's attention, pulling at his shirt and babbling away in a staccato-paced recitation. They moved down the hall together and to a door on the left that led to the living room. Two sofa beds lined the walls and a dining table and chairs filled the opposite end by a lace-curtained window that looked out over the city. In the distance, Marielle could see the looming tower of the Palace of Culture. At the table sat a tall woman in her fifties who, despite her simple skirt and blouse, had an elegant bearing. Her dark hair, with no sign of gray, was pulled back in a French knot.

She rose and stretched out her hand to Marielle.

"I am Halina Marek, mother of Tomas, sister of Janosch, who tells me many things of your family and your vineyards," she said in German. "My sympathy at the loss of your father. Janosch had great respect and love for him."

Marielle took her hand and returned the firm grasp, knowing that Halina, while gracious, was measuring her. Marielle had no doubt that Halina, like her own mother, had recognized the depth of Tomas's feelings.

She was acutely conscious of her position as an intruder in this house full of women—all of whom had their own special connection to Tomas. She wondered if he was equally aware, or oblivious to the impact of her presence here.

She glanced around the cramped space and wondered if she and Tomas would find the privacy to explore the physical closeness they'd tasted at the Central Station. Perhaps she should've insisted on booking a hotel when he'd first suggested she come. She hadn't wanted to impose on their hospitality; now she felt even more the disruption that her visit was causing.

But her concerns were postponed by the noisy bustling of Nyanya, who marched into the room with a steaming soup tureen.

"Zupa!" she declared, depositing the bowl on the table and gesturing for everyone to sit.

After the meal, Marielle distributed her gifts. Magdalena became absorbed in dressing and undressing the doll. Halina expressed appreciation for her thoughtfulness and Nyanya clucked over the shawl but was more thrilled with the food. She told Marielle through Tomas that she would now be able to prepare a feast with what Marielle had brought.

Marielle volunteered to help her, an offer that was noted but refused by the old woman. She did allow Marielle to carry the packages into the kitchen and Marielle then understood that it was Nyanya's domain. The narrow room had barely enough space for one person to work. In one corner was a bed that had been the old woman's since she'd arrived from the countryside thirty years before to care for the infant Tomas. Under the bed were all her worldly possessions, stored in salvaged cardboard boxes and fastened with saved string.

Tomas and Marielle spent the afternoon in the park with Magdalena, who persisted in her reluctance to talk to Marielle. When prompted, she had whispered a barely audible *"Dziekuję"* for the gifts earlier in the day. Marielle waited on a bench and watched as Tomas pushed Magdalena on the swings and caught her as she slid down the slide countless times. She took pleasure in observing Tomas with his daughter. His affection for her, expressed in small gestures of tenderness, caught in Marielle's throat. She thought of his hands earlier that day, grazing her softly as he led her out of the station, caressing her on the tram, lifting her firmly to bring her level with his eyes and his longing. She had no idea when or how she would feel his hands in such intimacy again. She knew she wanted that—and more. She also knew that the devotion she was witnessing between Tomas and Magdalena, a devotion she understood to her core, closed off even the glimmer of hope that she and Tomas might have a future together. Tomas would never leave Magdalena. And the regime would never allow Magdalena to leave Poland.

Marielle bit her lip and forced back the tears that were too close to the surface. She would not mar the three days she had on her visa by wallowing in what was denied to her. She got up from the bench and found a piece of chalk by the edge of the playground's asphalt surface. Kneeling, she sketched out the boxes for hopscotch, then searched the bare ground for a flat stone.

Curious, Magdalena watched her. Marielle offered her the stone but she shook her head and hid behind Tomas. Tomas took the stone instead and tossed it on the first square. He began hopping, much to the amusement of both Magdalena and Marielle. When he missed, he handed the stone to his daughter and she began to play. But when her turn was over she handed the stone back to Tomas.

"Nie!" He shook his head and pointed to Marielle. "It's Marielle's turn!"

Marielle held her breath, half expecting the girl to throw the stone on the ground and stalk away. But something in her father's tone clearly warned her that was not acceptable. She reluctantly held the stone out to Marielle, and Marielle smiled at her.

"Dziekuję."

The girl turned to her father. "She speaks Polish?"

"She's trying. Maybe you can teach her."

They finished the game, with Magdalena pointing to the various squares and repeating the numbers for Marielle, who stumbled through their pronunciation.

On the walk back to the apartment they counted in singsong, Magdalena riding on Tomas's shoulders.

After supper that evening, Tomas explained the sleeping arrangements. Marielle was to have the single bedroom, normally occupied by Halina and Magdalena.

They would sleep on the sofa beds in the living room and Tomas planned to sleep at a neighbor's on the floor below. Marielle, dismayed at the disruption, insisted on sleeping on the sofa and allowing Halina and Magdalena to stay in their bedroom. Despite much protesting and insistence, it was finally settled when it became clear that the little girl needed her own bed to fall asleep. After she was settled, Janosch joined them and Halina brought out a bottle of vodka and four narrow glasses.

"It's not Riesling, but it's our national drink," she said, as they toasted the friendship between the two families.

Around midnight Janosch took his leave and Halina said good-night. Nyanya had long before closed the kitchen door, muttered her prayers and turned out the light.

Tomas smiled at Marielle.

"You've survived your first day."

"Are you surprised?"

"No. I expected you to charm all of them. And though you may not believe it or realize it, you have."

He took a step toward her and pulled her to him. She felt the warmth of his breath on her neck, the security of his arms around her, his lean body against her own. He kissed her slowly, so many times that she lost count, and once again found herself melting into him, rigidity giving way to a softness and a willingness that was new to her. She had never known herself to be so pliant. She felt him slip his arm under her and carry her to the bed. For an instant he left her there and she was bereft, but he had moved away only to turn off the light. The immediate darkness was total. No streetlights burned outside the apartment to cast even a hazy illumination through the window and there was no moon. She felt him before he was close enough to see the outline of his face. He stretched his body the length of hers and pulled the duvet over them. Despite the April date, temperatures still dropped at night and they'd shut off the heater hours before to conserve fuel. Warmth spread through her from his closeness and her own surging blood. He began to kiss her again in silence, and then moved his hands down her body.

Marielle wasn't without experience with men. She had had a steady boyfriend in university and had stumbled through the awkward couplings that had come at the end of long hours of studying or Saturday-evening gatherings where too much alcohol had been consumed. After graduation they'd drifted apart, especially when Marielle had gotten the prestigious offer from Deutsche Bank. For a while she'd dated another expatriate while she was living in Hong Kong. But neither relationship had prepared her for the emotional intensity of her feelings for Tomas. She felt as if every nerve ending in her skin was alive, every brain cell was firing in joy. Every part of her body—muscle, skin, blood—was attuned to this moment and Tomas's nearness. Although she'd been conscious of Nyanya's snoring behind the kitchen door and her ears had been alert for the sound of Magdalena waking from a dream, she now heard nothing but Tomas's steady breathing and his heart, beating beneath her hand.

They made love in silence, with only the gentle escape of a sigh as, freed from the layers of clothing and restraint they'd carried all day, their skin first made contact—belly to belly, legs wrapped around each other, arms taking each other in. In the past, Marielle had often felt as if she were outside her body when she'd had sex, watching herself go through the motions, responding to touch, following the lead of her partner, but never fully engaged. For the first time in her life, Marielle was no longer an observer, but lost in the midst of a deep pleasure that seemed to obliterate the distance she'd always kept between herself and others. She was surprised by how emboldened she was, how hungry for Tomas and his body. She pulled him into her, wrapping herself tightly around him, aware of her power as she felt him respond to her with a hunger as aching and desperate as her own.

She didn't know herself as she felt the boundaries between her body and his dissolve, ignoring the geographic and political boundaries that had dominated her thoughts in the weeks leading up to this night. Their lovemaking allowed her to forget, if only for these few hours, what separated them. Surrounded by the dark nothingness that disguised the limits of Tomas's life, she let those limits slip away—the bleak apartment block; the cramped flat crowded not just with furniture and belongings but also with the unfulfilled needs of the three people who loved Tomas so intently; the constant sense of struggle to meet even the most basic necessities of life. For a blissful few hours the darkness and the silence gave Marielle and Tomas only each other, because that was all they could perceive. Heartbeat, breath, lips, hands were their only reality.

They fell asleep briefly, their bodies slick with sweat beneath the comforter despite the chill in the room. At 3:00 a.m. they woke and made love again, but with a more bittersweet mood. He murmured that Nyanya would be awake soon and he'd have to at least make the pretense of having slept on his neighbor's sofa. He drew away, kissing her lips and then her forehead and then her now-tangled hair as he rose from the bed. He pulled on his pants and sweater and eased himself out the door of the apartment.

Marielle rolled over to where Tomas had lain, breathed in his familiar scent and hugged herself as she tried to close her eyes to the approaching dawn and the encroachments of Tomas's life.

Morning began early in the Marek household. It was Easter Sunday. Nyanya was up at five to begin preparations for the meal. By six, Magdalena was chattering to her grandmother and Marielle could hear through the thin walls the sound of drawers opening. She thought about remaining under the covers longer but sensed that Magdalena would soon be out of the bedroom. She feared that whatever tentative steps Magdalena had taken toward her yesterday would be obliterated in an instant if Magdalena came bounding over to the bed normally occupied by Tomas and found Marielle instead.

She threw back the comforter and forced herself up, taking the bathrobe she hadn't used the night before out of her suitcase and slipping it on just as Magdalena opened the bedroom door. Marielle, toothbrush in hand, was on her way to the bathroom as Magdalena scanned the room.

"Where's my papa?" she asked Marielle in Polish.

Although she understood the question, Marielle's grasp of the language wasn't enough to answer.

From the bedroom, Halina answered her granddaughter.

"He spent the night with Antony— Don't you remember he told you that when he kissed you goodnight? He'll be back soon and we'll all go to church. Come here now and I'll braid your hair."

"Not yet, Grandma. Breakfast, first," and she ran to the kitchen.

Marielle washed up quickly in the bathroom, cautious of the limited water supply, and dressed in the living room while Magdalena ate in the kitchen with Nyanya. She brushed the tangles out of her hair, braided it and then wrapped the braids around her head. She hadn't worn her hair like this since she was a little girl but something about the day and her sense of being pulled back in time by Warsaw drew her hands into the familiar pattern of braiding.

She made the bed and stored the pillows and linens in the storage compartment under the mattress. Smoothing down the skirt of her suit, she went into the kitchen.

It was warm with steam rising from the boiling potatoes. Cucumbers, peeled and sliced paper thin, were draining in a colander over the sink. A bowl of pastry dough covered with a kitchen towel was rising at the back of the stove. Nyanya gestured to the pot of coffee on the burner and got up to cut her a slice of bread. She held out an egg, as well, but Marielle replied with a "No, thank you."

Magdalena stared at her as she poured a cup of the thick coffee in the pot.

The little girl asked her something, but Marielle didn't understand.

"Nie rozumiem." I don't understand.

Magdalena jumped out of her seat and tugged at Marielle to stoop down to her level. When she did, she touched the braids circling Marielle's head.

"Who?"

Marielle pointed to herself. "I did."

Magdalena then ran from the room, calling to Halina. In a minute she was back with her hairbrush and bobby pins and thrust them into Marielle's hands. With an elaborate pantomime, she demonstrated that she wanted Marielle to braid her hair the same way.

When Nyanya realized what was going on, she shooed them out of the kitchen.

"No hair in here!" she scolded.

Marielle took her coffee and moved into the living room with Magdalena and sat beside her on the sofa. She was surprised the little girl wanted her attention, but she threw herself into the task, brushing out the tangles gently and then coaxing the wispy strands into neat braids. It was the first time she'd had such tactile contact with a child. With no siblings, she hadn't had the opportunity to be "Auntie" to anyone, and she had grown distant from the women she'd gone to high school with who now had children. It was comforting to have Magdalena so near, to smell her soapy fragrance and have her so clearly enjoying the work of Marielle's hands.

When she finished, she dug a compact out of her purse, opened it and put the mirror in Magdalena's hands so she could see the braids. Magdalena touched the side of her head and beamed.

At that moment Tomas entered the apartment. He was brought to a standstill by the sight of Marielle and Magdalena side by side with the same hairstyle— Marielle's a deep chestnut and Magdalena's golden.

"Good morning, my ladies," he said, his eyes lingering on Marielle as the color rose in her cheeks. She wasn't sure how she'd get through the day when she felt a sense memory sweep over her body as Tomas took her in with his eyes.

"Papa, look at my hair! Just like Janina and Kasia." She twirled around.

"You look like a very grown-up young lady. Grandma must be very happy that you sat still long enough for her to braid it."

"Grandma didn't do it! *She* did."

"Marielle? Did you thank her for such a beautiful job?" Halina had come into the room and touched Magdalena's braids. She held a circle of brightly colored artificial flowers decorated with blue ribbons.

"Dziekuję," murmured Magdalena.

"Would you like to wear the flowers to church?" Halina set the flowers on her head and Magdalena fidgeted with them till they fit comfortably.

"Now you look like a proper young Polish lady."

Together, the whole family, including Nyanya in her black dress, walked to church, Magdalena's ribbons bobbing as she hurried to keep pace with the adults. The service was long and Marielle was fascinated by the devotion of the congregants. Unlike in Germany, the church wasn't filled only with old women. Young families, couples, groups spanning generations like the Mareks, crowded the pews and spilled into the side aisles. It was a revelation to Marielle that the church was so viable here. Although she didn't understand a word of the sermon, she recognized the passion of the priest in the pulpit and watched the rapt faces around her, the people nodding as he spoke. She watched Tomas, as well, tracing with her eyes the planes of his face and body that she'd caressed the night before with her hands.

After church, Marielle helped Halina set the table while Nyanya finished the meal and Tomas and Magdalena played a game of checkers in the bedroom.

"He has so little time with her, he must make the most of the weekends," Halina confided. "It's never enough for her. She's afraid of losing him the way she lost her mother."

It was the first mention of Tomas's wife. Marielle was

torn between wanting to know and wanting to deny her existence. In the end, she decided that she needed to know.

"How?" she asked.

"She left for work one day and didn't come back. Magdalena was four—old enough to question, to believe somehow that it was her fault. My daughter-in-law was a troubled young woman and she suffered mentally. Tomas searched for her for many months, forgetting himself, forgetting his child, blaming himself for something he couldn't fix."

"Did he find her?" Marielle realized she wanted the answer to be yes, wanted Tomas to have that emptiness behind him, wanted him to be free to love *her*.

"He did. She was destroying herself with drugs. She'd been a nurse and so had easy access to painkillers, which she'd started to take to kill the pain in her spirit. In the end, they killed her, as well. Tomas brought her home, got her help, but she overdosed—about a year ago now. Thank God, not here, not in front of her child. They found her under a bridge on the outskirts of Ujazdowski Park."

Marielle was very still. The suffering of this family and their ability to put one foot in front of the other and continue was incredible.

"I'm so sorry, Halina. Thank you for telling me. It explains so much."

"I wouldn't have told you, wouldn't have betrayed my son's privacy, if I hadn't witnessed what has passed between you in this short time. Tomas does not know how to protect himself in love. He suffered greatly with the loss of Krystyna. I can't bear to have him suffer again. I want you to understand that before you go any deeper into this relationship. He will not abandon his child."

"I know that, Halina. I will never ask that of him."

"Unless you abandon your mother and your vineyards, I don't understand what you two are doing to each other."

"I don't understand, either. But I've never loved anyone the way I love Tomas."

"Then God help you both."

CHAPTER NINE

At two in the afternoon, Janosch arrived with his wife, their daughter and her husband and their two little girls, Janina and Kasia, whose hairstyle Magdalena had been delighted to emulate. The family crowded around the table and ate and drank, including the newly bottled wine Marielle had brought from the 1975 harvest—a wine that would soon be described as "phenomenal" by experts. The meal stretched out over several hours, with vigorous discussions punctuating the gaps between the courses. Nyanya clucked over everyone and smiled with satisfaction at the feast she'd produced with the gifts Marielle had carried across the border and provisions obtained through her own bartering and haggling. Tomas had told Marielle how Nyanya would head out of the apartment in the morning with an empty net bag and some treasure she could trade. She traveled across the city on three trolleys to the bazaar and negotiated and cajoled at open stalls for black market meat and fruits that were not to be had with ration coupons at the government stores. Somehow, she'd always managed to feed them, even when shortages and soaring prices had put the most basic necessities out of reach. Her pride at this Easter meal was palpable, and the family was rewarding her with the highest praise—their vociferous enjoyment of everything she put on the table. Pierogi stuffed with potatoes and cheese, wild mushroom soup, ham, potatoes baked with eggs and sour cream, stuffed cabbage, and for dessert, pastry twists and cheesecake.

It was past eleven when the last of the pastries had been eaten, the vodka bottle was empty and the three little girls had fallen asleep on the sofa. Janosch and his son-in-law each carried one of the cousins down to the car. Halina carefully slipped Magdalena's dirndl off and tucked her into bed while Marielle and Tomas cleared the remnants from the table.

By midnight Nyanya had turned off the light in the kitchen and closed the door. Halina bid them goodnight, but with a penetrating glance at Marielle that Tomas didn't miss.

"What was that look for?"

"She's a mother who loves her son and doesn't want to see him hurt."

"Does she think you're going to hurt me?"

"She thinks we're hurting each other—that it's madness to continue this relationship when we can't be together."

"Is that what you believe?"

"I did in the beginning. No, wait. I still think it's madness. But I can't stop loving you. It's too late."

"It's too late for me, as well."

He took her in his arms. Their lovemaking that night had an elegiac quality to it, a consciousness that this touch, that kiss, would be the last for many months. Marielle wanted to commit to memory the sound of his voice whispering her name, the hollows of his body into which her curves fit, the scents of both of them mingled on his skin. She clung to him afterward, unable to sleep or to let him go until it was nearly dawn.

In the morning, Marielle said goodbye to the three women. Nyanya blessed her and put a small packet of herbs in her hand.

"For the *zupa*," she directed.

Magdalena kissed her on the cheek and stepped back. Halina embraced her silently.

With Tomas, she reversed her trip of Saturday morning, traveling by trolley to the city center and the train station. Tomas had arranged with the clinic to have the morning off so he could spend these last few hours with her. They sat in silence in the stuffy trolley, a light rain spattering the windows. He held her hand.

"Thank you for coming. It was a lot to ask."

"Thank you for asking. There was nowhere else I wanted to be." She hesitated, then asked the question that was hovering between them.

"Will you come for the harvest?"

"Yes."

She nodded. They rode in silence again until the transfer point, where they changed lines.

"Is this what our lives will be from now on? A few days of bliss each year punctuating a lonely existence?"

"I won't ask you to do that. I've been lonely for a long time, even before my wife's death. I'm used to it. My time with you is a gift. But you—you have a world of opportunity before you. The vineyards, your friends. Your life is full of possibilities. Don't close yourself off to those possibilities because of me."

She turned to him.

"There is no possibility for me except you."

A look of both pain and hope skimmed across Tomas's face as she spoke.

"It's too much to ask of you," he protested.

"It's too much to ask me to let you go. I don't know what else to do except wait for the harvest and store up from our time together what will sustain us for the rest of the year."

She kissed him as the trolley pulled into the station—a firm, determined, decisive kiss. There was no more to say. No other solution.

They parted on the platform as the final boarding call for the train to Prague was announced. He held her against him. He buried his face in the scent of her hair, still in its braids. She leaned into his chest, pressing her ear one last time to the steady rhythm of his heart.

Once on the train she took a window seat and watched for as long as he was visible. He remained on the platform until the last car had made the bend beyond the station. Then he turned and walked back into his life.

CHAPTER TEN

1976-1982

TOMAS AND JANOSCH and the crew returned in the fall for the next harvest. Marielle had renovated an unused wing of the winery in the ell over the tank room, turning it into an apartment for herself. It was there that she intended to live with Tomas for the six weeks of the harvest. She anticipated Anita's objection. The village was small; opinions of the Polish workers among the older members of the community were often negative. Even though the entrance to the apartment was within the enclosed courtyard and not on the street, Marielle knew it wouldn't be long before the gossips began chattering over loaves of bread at Ute's bakery.

She braced herself for the conversation with her mother as they painted the new rooms in late August.

"Mama, I want you to know my intentions when Tomas arrives in October. I'm going to invite him to stay here instead of at the campground."

"That's gracious of you to wait to move in until after

the harvest. Why not ask Janosch, too? I'm sure he'd appreciate not having to live in that cramped tin box."

"Mama, this is difficult to explain. I mean to invite Tomas to stay *with me* in the apartment."

Anita put down the paintbrush and looked at her daughter.

"Do you realize what you're exposing yourself to? Not only the criticism of the village, but a weakening of your position with the crew! You're the chief, they're the workers. To be so blatant about your relationship with Tomas is damaging to your authority. It's suicidal."

"Mama, this whole relationship is suicidal. I can't live with him. I can't live without him. At least for these few short weeks, I intend to give us the life we can never have!"

"It's a pretense. A fairy tale. You shouldn't flaunt it. I'm not telling you to stop loving him. Believe me, I understand. But don't live with him while he's here. This isn't the anonymity of Frankfurt. You'll suffer in subtle ways because of the judgment of others. Listen to me, Marielle."

Reluctantly, Marielle acquiesced to Anita's advice. She asked Tomas and Janosch to stay in the apartment and gave up her fantasy of a few weeks of domestic life. But the apartment connected via an internal door to the main part of the house, and both Anita and Janosch ignored Tomas's nightly visit to Marielle's bedroom.

They deepened their intimacy during those nights— sometimes simply falling asleep in each other's arms, physically exhausted by the day's labor. Sometimes they continued conversations that had begun earlier in the evening, about the vineyards, about Magdalena and, as the end of the harvest approached, about their relationship.

Tomas continued to struggle with his belief that he was cutting Marielle off from the chance to live a full live—with a husband and a family.

"I'm not sure I ever saw that as the direction my life would take, especially when I set out on my career at Deutsche Bank. Now that I'm responsible for the winery, my life is full. The vineyards are my children. I'm not missing anything in my life because of you. On the contrary, you're filling an emptiness that had been there for a long time.

"Tomas, I'm not going to deny that there's nothing I want more than to be your wife. But that isn't within my reach. Perhaps we *can't* make this work. But I'm as committed to you as if I wore your ring."

Tomas left that year, as he had in the past, on the morning after St. Martin's Day. They watched the flames of the bonfire together, his arm lightly around her waist, grateful for these last moments together and the ritual of the fire, warming them as the darkness and the winter of separation closed in on them.

Tomas returned for two more harvests without another visit by Marielle to Warsaw. Anita finally relented the third time and no longer cautioned Marielle about the propriety of his living with her during the harvest. She'd witnessed the constancy between them during their annual separations—letters weekly and always, on Valentine's Day, a huge bouquet of roses, delivered first thing in the morning by Maria.

When Karol Wojtyla, the archbishop of Kraków, was elected as Pope John Paul II in 1978, a new energy and sense of identity surged in Poland. In 1979, Marielle returned to Poland at the same time as the pope. When he knelt on the tarmac at the airport and kissed the ground of his homeland, Marielle understood the emotional meaning of this visit and acknowledged her own connection to Poland. As it did for John Paul II, a piece of her heart remained on Polish soil, even though her life's work and responsibilities lay elsewhere.

With thousands of other people, but conscious only of the man by her side, Marielle experienced one of the pope's outdoor Masses and began to grasp what she'd observed at the church on Easter Sunday a few years before. For Poles, the Church was more than devotion and prayer. It was the constant that defined them despite a turbulent history of shifting borders and foreign oppression. With this second visit, Marielle fit another piece into the puzzle of understanding Tomas.

During the months of separation between harvests, Marielle accumulated more puzzle pieces in the form of Tomas's letters. They were a journal, recounting the minutiae of his life in a way that allowed Marielle to imagine his daily existence. As she moved through her own life, pruning, planting, rushing to the hillside after a particularly devastating storm to survey the damage to the vines, she would sometimes pause and see him—treating patients at the clinic, seated at the dining table with Halina and Magdalena in the evening, attending a recital when Magdalena began studying the violin. It was reassuring to know that he was living in a world parallel to hers.

As the date of the harvest approached, however, she would develop a heightened emotional state. Despite the letters, she always felt a stab of uncertainty. Each year was as if they were beginning anew, with an initial reserve that marked the first day of his arrival. Tomas and Janosch always came to dinner the first night, a meal Marielle prepared with great care. She drove into Wiesbaden to the food market in the lower level of the Carsch-Haus department store and selected meat and produce from the abundant displays at each stall. One year she made duck roasted with apples, raisins and sauerkraut that had been braised in Riesling. Another time she chose a leg of lamb that she simmered with onions and bacon in a sauce made from broth and Burgundy and served with dumplings.

In some ways, the elaborate preparations for the meal and the ritual of the meal itself eased the transition from life without Tomas to Tomas as a daily presence. She poured her energy into chopping and peeling and stirring to still the voices in her head, the questions about how Tomas would react to her when he walked through the door.

Each time he arrived, he greeted Anita first—in the early years with a simple handshake and later with a kiss on each cheek that she warmly returned. Then he took Marielle in his arms and bent to kiss her, holding her with his eyes closed for a moment as they both relished the reunion.

Their first night together always began tentatively, an exploration of achingly familiar territory. But as their bodies grew comfortable with each other again, their hesitancy gave way to a recklessness and abandon and outpouring of all that had been pent up during their months of separation.

For seven years these reunions repeated themselves, sustaining their love. Marielle's wines were gaining attention as she grew in confidence and knowledge in her winemaking. Magdalena turned thirteen during Solidarity's revolutionary impact on Poland and was developing into a bright and motivated student. Tomas was named head of surgery at the hospital.

CHAPTER ELEVEN

1983-1988

IN THE SPRING OF 1983, Marielle came face-to-face with the consequences of the choice she'd made to lead this divided and often incomplete life. The Rheingau Vintners' Association arranged a trip for the group to travel to the Mosel region to visit the vineyards of a similar group of vintners. Marielle, at Anita's encouragement, decided to go. It was a valuable opportunity to learn new techniques and be exposed to new ideas. It was also more fun than Marielle had had in a long time.

She realized how narrow her world had become in the years since she hadtaken over the winery. She had devoted herself to the business and only making time for Tomas, writing to him every week. Her friends from Frankfurt had long since moved on in their lives—furthering their own careers at the bank, starting families. Relaxing for a few days with colleagues who shared the same challenges was a delightful respite. She laughed, hiked through glorious countryside and sat over lingering meals with a different wine for each course.

She also met a man. Klaus Eckhardt ran a winery in Kiedrich, about twenty kilometers north of her village. He was about forty, an outgoing and energetic man who reminded her in many ways of her father. There was an earthiness and frankness to him—a man without pretense who considered himself first and foremost a farmer. He sat next to her on the bus and entertained her with hilarious stories of his education as a vintner. His stories put her own anxieties in perspective. When the trip was over, Klaus invited her to a concert at Kloster Eberbach, an ancient monastery with extraordinary acoustics.

Again, Marielle had a wonderful time in his company, forgetting her loneliness and the stress of business. He had a large extended family full of nieces and nephews, the children of his six brothers and sisters. Marielle felt herself absorbed with ease into Klaus's noisy and comfortable family. One summer evening she sat on his brother's veranda, watching the sunset as the adults enjoyed a bottle of Klaus's Spätburgunder and the children played on the lawn.

It was a scene she hadn't expected to be part of, and she was disturbed by prickles of dissatisfaction. She hadn't thought she wanted something as prosaic as this—a traditional vision of family life. It surprised her to be feeling this lack, and she went home that evening wondering if she would ever regret not marrying and having children.

She felt no physical attraction to Klaus, but she appreciated his humor and warmth. He became a friend, willing to coax her out of her driven focus on work. She even told him about Tomas.

All summer she questioned what might be missing from her life. She noticed women pushing strollers. When it was her turn to host the tasting stand at the village park she watched families walking, children on bikes, grandmothers doting on grandchildren. Was this a buried need she'd put aside? Would it haunt her? She didn't know.

When Tomas came in October, he was thinner and more worn than she'd ever seen him. Martial law had been imposed in the wake of strikes; civil liberties had been suspended and many union leaders imprisoned. His hospital had received many of the injured when government troops had attacked striking laborers. Once again, Poland had been in economic and political crisis. Marielle saw the human effect of the turmoil in Poland every time the crew arrived in the fall, but Tomas seemed to embody the ravages of failed policies more acutely than the others. When she took him into her bed the first night, she felt the unprotected angles of his body and sought to surround him with her own softness and comfort.

After a few weeks of work in the open air and Anita's hearty meals, he'd lost his gauntness. In his arms, Marielle felt his strength once again.

"Are you happy?" he asked her late one night after lovemaking.

"Yes," she said. "Being here with you is what makes my life meaningful."

"But is it enough? I look at you, how hard you work. And I see very little else, except waiting for these few weeks. You should be living, not waiting."

"When you're here, I forget the waiting."

"But when I'm not here…"

He always seemed to be attuned to what she was thinking, despite her efforts to protect him from her doubts.

"Marielle, you're still a young woman, young enough to start a family. You're living half a life."

"I didn't think I needed the other half until…"

"Until what? Until someone?"

"Not someone in the way you mean. I'm not in love with anyone else. But I was introduced to a family this year, with children and grandparents and uncles and aunts, and I didn't know until I was in the midst of it that it represented a hole in my life."

"You could come to Poland and have that." His voice was pained. He knew she wasn't free to say yes, no matter how much she wanted that, wanted him.

She knew he wished he could give her a whole life. She still didn't know how to define that life.

They didn't resolve their dilemma that night. It hovered over them throughout the harvest and imbued their lovemaking with a desperation and hunger that drove them to a level of intensity that echoed their first time in Warsaw.

They exhausted themselves physically and emotionally. They talked in each other's arms, over the dinner table, during long walks on Sunday mornings along the river's edge.

As the Feast of St. Martin approached, Tomas came to a decision. He'd seen the look on Marielle's face on Sundays when they passed families on the river path, a look she struggled to mask. But he knew her too well.

Like the centurion giving up his red cloak to the shivering beggar, Tomas gave up his claim to Marielle's heart.

"I need to set you free, Marielle. This is no life for you. Find what you need. Don't wake up twenty years from now full of regret and bitter that I couldn't let you go."

He left, as he always did, early the next morning. He kissed her for the last time and closed the gate to the courtyard behind him.

The rhythm of her life for the last eight years an the way she defined herself were disrupted, torn. For weeks, she went through the motions of running the winery and did nothing else. Klaus called to invite her to the Kiedricher Advent concert. He'd been busy with his own harvest, but had also kept his distance when Tomas was there. She accepted the invitation and was swept back into Klaus's exuberant family. For a few months she entertained the idea of considering Klaus romantically, but when she couldn't imagine herself making love to him, she gently dissuaded him from his hopes that they could ever be a couple.

Gradually she opened herself up to meeting other men. Matchmaking friends of Anita's began to set up blind dates. She dutifully attempted to make conversation over dinners up and down the Rheingau. Now and then she went on a second date. For a while she was serious with a young research scientist who shared her interest in rowing. She felt a "normalcy" to her social life.

But she missed Tomas even more than she'd expected. His empathy, his intensity, his tenderness, his understanding of who she was beneath the facade of smart, driven businesswoman.

In the fall, Tomas continued to return for the harvest, but he didn't work with Marielle. Instead he joined a crew working another vineyard, the one where he'd labored as a teenager. His path and Marielle's did not cross.

For four years, Marielle thought her desire for a family would override the reservations she had about one man or another. But she found that she couldn't will herself to love. Whenever she got close enough, she saw only what the men couldn't give her. In the winter of 1987 she received a proposal of marriage and turned it down. She spent the following spring and summer alone, deliberately withdrawing from the dating scene. She was in retreat from partnership and coupling.

During that time she reread the hundreds of letters Tomas had written her over the years of their relationship. She sat up in bed at night, remembering and reliving.

She remembered, as well, his final conversation with her. "Don't look back with regret twenty years from now."

In October, after Janosch and the crew arrived, she

drove to the campground the first Sunday morning and knocked on the door of the camper. Tomas answered.

His hair was beginning to gray and the lines around his eyes had deepened. His hands, hanging at his sides, were still beautiful.

"I have no regrets," she said. "I want you in my life however and whenever you can be there."

She held her breath. She had no idea what had filled Tomas's life in the four years they'd been apart. Had he found a woman who could be wife and mother in Poland?

He reached out his hand and stroked the side of her face, then gathered her into his arms, burying a moan in the hollow of her neck. She sobbed, her tears spilling onto his shoulder.

CHAPTER TWELVE

November 1989

IN 1989 WHEN TOMAS came back for the harvest, he once again moved into Marielle's apartment. In the evenings, instead of struggling to learn her craft as she had so many years before, Marielle painted. That fall, rather than her usual landscape, she painted Tomas's portrait.

She finished it in the beginning of November and brought it to a shop in Wiesbaden to be framed. On November 9 she drove into the city to pick it up and take care of other errands. She was on her way home when she turned on the car radio to catch the weather report.

The news was on, and the announcer's voice was heightened, incredulous, jubilant. Marielle stopped her car and pulled over.

"Die Mauer ist weg!" The Berlin Wall had fallen.

Marielle was numb, disbelieving. She switched radio stations, thinking she'd misheard or the reporter had made a mistake. But every station was reporting the same thing.

Trembling, she drove home, pulling the car into the courtyard and racing up the stairs to the apartment.

"Have you heard?" She burst into the apartment. Tomas, sitting in front of the television, nodded. He stood up and she ran to him, still trembling—because of what this meant for East and West Germany, for Eastern Europe, for them.

THE MONTHS THAT followed were marked by hope, upheaval and a disruption of old ways and limited expectations. As welcome as the extraordinary change was in their lives and their definition of home, country, Europe, it was change nonetheless.

The patterns they'd established, the rituals and boundaries that protected all of them, not just Tomas and Marielle, but those they loved—Magdalena, Halina, Nyanya, Anita—it all began to shift. Like a handful of loose rocks, skittering down the hillside, barely noticeable as they tumbled over closely cropped grass and carefully tended rows of vines. But the changes gathered momentum over the winter, like the muddy landslide set off by the heavy, unrelenting rains so long ago.

Marielle and Anita went to Warsaw for Christmas. Magdalena, twenty-one and in her second year of studies at Jagiellonian University, arrived home on the same day. Her hair was closely cropped and spiked, its little-girl blondness heightened to a near-platinum shade. She wore American jeans and smoked French cigarettes and now used the name "Maggi." Nyanya chased her out to the balcony when she pulled out her cigarettes, scolding and complaining about what she'd become.

At dinner on *Wigilia,* Christmas Eve, the Oplatek—the blessed bread—was passed from hand to hand, each of them taking a fragment as the first star appeared in the night sky.

"I have an announcement." Maggi held her vodka glass high, as if she was about to make a toast. "I've been accepted to an exchange program at Juilliard in America. I start next September."

Everyone's glass went up in congratulations. Nyanya wiped her eyes with her napkin, her expression a mixture of pride in Magdalena's accomplishment combined with puzzlement and loss. Tomas looked at his daughter with eyes that revealed his surprise—not at her announcement, because she'd confided in him that she'd applied to the conservatory. His surprise was his sudden recognition of Magdalena's confidence in her future, her embrace of the freedom she now had to define her life however she chose.

How had that fact escaped him? For so long he'd been consumed with sheltering her, surrounding her with love to cushion her from the loss of her mother. That his love and protection could have formed her into a bird with such strong wings and an even stronger desire to fly was a revelation to him that night.

It was the moment he realized that she'd surpassed him, that she no longer needed him. And he was free.

On Christmas, a day of brilliant sunshine and biting cold, Tomas and Marielle walked home from church, their arms linked and their heads wrapped in wool scarves.

"I want to talk with you apart from the others," he said. "Let's stop in the park for a few minutes."

They sat facing each other on a wooden bench that was free of snow.

"Magdalena's announcement last night cleared my head of a worry I hadn't even known I was carrying. I think I finally saw her as a woman, eager to leap into this new world that's opening up for her generation. It made me feel old, but at the same time I rejoiced for her." He looked away, his vulnerability palpable.

Marielle stroked the side of his cheek with her gloved hand and smiled.

"It also made me see that there's nothing to hold me back now, and it frightens me a little. I feel like an old woman who's become so used to limitations that I cannot imagine any other kind of life. Until my daughter opened the door for me in a way the hole in the Berlin wall did not."

He placed his hand over Marielle's.

"Marry me, Marielle. Let me give you the complete man. On your soil."

At dinner that afternoon they made their own announcement to the family and invited them all to the winery on Valentine's Day for the wedding.

In February, Maggi drove Halina and Nyanya across the boundaries that for so many years had been ominous barriers. Tomas had gone ahead, to begin looking for work and to start the paperwork to be licensed as a physician in Germany.

Marielle asked Maggi to be her maid of honor and took her shopping in Wiesbaden to find a dress that would both suit her nontraditional style and be something she'd want to take to America in the fall. They spent an afternoon wandering in and out of small shops and department stores. As Maggi delighted in the selection of fabrics and the choices arrayed on the racks, Marielle watched her and saw not only herself at that age but the daughter she'd never had.

Maggi's final choice was a black jersey wrap dress that was a striking counterpoint to her blondness and pale skin. Neither Halina nor Nyanya approved of its color or style—they would've preferred to see her as Magdalena, still in her traditional dirndl. But Marielle, about to become her mother, overruled their objections.

The villages of the Rheingau were preparing for Fasching, the German celebration of Carneval in the weeks leading up to Lent. Parades wound their way through the streets with floats full of costumed revelers tossing candy to children. Streamers of multicolored confetti flew through the air. It was a time of abandon in those first months of 1990, and Marielle and Tomas found themselves swept up in the music and the gaiety.

The morning of the wedding, Maria arrived with her usual delivery of Valentine roses, but instead of the dozen Tomas had always ordered in the past, he'd requested ten times as many. Maria had combed the wholesale flower market in Frankfurt, corralling as many of the deep burgundy blooms as she could find.

The winery's public rooms were ablaze with color, with bowls of roses on every table, set for the guests who would celebrate with them later in the day. Vases also rested on the windowsills formed by the meter-thick walls.

Rather than wear white, Marielle chose a dress the color of the roses, its velvet fabric echoing their texture. Her bouquet, in contrast, was white, with a single red rose at its center. She pinned another single rose to Tomas's lapel before they walked to the church.

During the wedding ceremony, Maggi played her violin for them, a vibrant and inventive rendition of "Spring" from Vivaldi's *Four Seasons.* Marielle felt the world coming to life for her and Tomas in those intense moments of music.

When they left the church on foot, followed by their guests, Maggi again put the violin to her chin and played as they strolled through the village to the winery. Along the way, friends opened windows and threw confetti and streamers. By the time they arrived at the gate to the courtyard, Marielle's hair was entwined with the mul-ticolored paper strands and Tomas's shoulders were covered with a dusting of confetti. At the reception they toasted each other and their guests with the 1988 Mar-cobruun, an extraordinary vintage that was to launch an incredible streak lasting eight years of great wines from the Rheingau.

Later that evening, as they lay in one another's arms for the first time as husband and wife, Tomas raised himself on one elbow and with his other hand traced circles on Marielle's belly.

"I've watched you in the last few days, taking on the role of Magdalena's mother as well as my wife, and I've thought how wonderful you are at it. A natural."

"Thank you." She kissed him.

"So I took that another step. What if we have a child

now? You and I. You're only forty-one. I know you gave that up for me but, like everything else we thought we'd forsaken—a life together, a future—we have a second chance. Why not?"

Marielle was still. A list of objections began to form in her mind, conditioned for so long not to want or imagine what she couldn't have.

But she knew that she'd never completely abandoned her desire to have a child. For Tomas, with his daughter grown, to offer her this gift overwhelmed her.

She burst into tears.

"Yes," she gulped, between sobs.

CHAPTER THIRTEEN

1991–2007

VALENTIN MAREK was born a year later, on Valentine's Day, doubly blessing the day for them.

During the harvest of 1991, Valentin slept in a backpack borne alternately by his mother and father, the rhythm of their movements lulling him in the crisp air.

By the harvest of 1995, he followed his great-uncle Janosch around, dumping buckets of grapes into Janosch's carrier as the old man stooped to Valentin's height. By the harvest of 1998, Valentin had his own shears and worked the lower layers of the vines, only occasionally popping a handful of grapes into his mouth.

Maggi, when she finished her studies at Juilliard, won a seat with the Berlin Philharmonic. When her concert schedule allowed, she came back for the harvest, and she always made time in the summers to perform with Tomas in the courtyard concerts that had become signature events for the winery. In 2000 she made her first solo recording and Tomas and Marielle hosted a launch party for her at the winery.

By the time he was thirteen in 2004, Valentin was as tall as his father, with the same long fingers. He had inherited his mother's eyes and chestnut hair, which he wore in dreadlocks, much to Anita's dismay. He'd also inherited Marielle's intensity, and was the winery's mechanic, fascinated by its equipment. He was less fascinated with school, and was chafing at the prospect of spending six more years preparing for the *Abitur* and then university, as his parents and his sister had before him.

On his sixteenth birthday he listened to the toasts of his parents and two grandmothers, made with wine from the case that had been set aside in his birth year. Each major event in his life—his baptism, his first day of school, his first communion—had been celebrated with the opening of a bottle from that case. On the occasion of his sixteenth birthday Marielle poured a small glass for him, as well. After the toasts, Valentin stood, brushing back the hair from his eyes.

"I have a birthday wish," he said solemnly. "It's something I've been thinking about for a while. I don't want to go to university."

He waited for the predictable objections, and his grandmothers did not disappoint. But Marielle and Tomas knew their son well enough to understand that something else was coming. They exchanged glances.

"I want to study winemaking instead. Maggi certainly isn't going to come back and take on the work, so who else but me?"

Marielle wanted to tell him it wasn't an expectation,

that he was free to make his own way in life, even if that took him away from the land. But Tomas squeezed her hand and she let Valentin go on.

"If you'll agree, I can transfer to the wine institute in the fall. I'm not interested in spending years in a classroom like you two did. I'm much happier working with my hands—repairing the tractor, rigging the bottler, pruning and grafting the vines.

"I'm not like you, Papa. I don't have the patience to study for years and years. And, Mama, I'll probably have to hire somebody to do the books when you've had enough of them. But I think I can make our hills flourish. What do you say?"

Marielle rose from the table and hugged him. Anita wiped her eyes. Even Halina was mollified.

Later that night, Tomas and Marielle took a walk. The moon was full, and sharing their anniversary with their son's birthday had led them to take time for themselves at the end of the day. The night was cold but clear and they headed up the vineyard path to the top of the hill.

Tomas kissed her, taking her face in his hands. "You've raised quite a young man, Mrs. Marek."

"So have you, Dr. Marek."

"No disappointments?"

"None. He's much more sure of himself than I was at his age."

Tomas nodded. "And much happier than I was."

"Are you happy now, Tomas?"

"Happier than I've ever been."

Silhouette® Desire

Silhouette® Desire

You can lead a horse to water...

When Alyssa Barkley and Clint Westmoreland
found out that their "fake" marriage was never
rendered void, they are forced to live together
for thirty days. However, Clint loves the single
life and has no intention of being tamed, but
when Alyssa moves in, the sizzling attraction
between them is ignited and neither wants the
thirty days to end.

Look for
TAMING CLINT WESTMORELAND
by
BRENDA JACKSON

Available February wherever you buy books

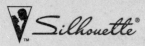

Romantic
SUSPENSE

**Sparked by Danger,
Fueled by Passion.**

When Tech Sergeant Jacob "Mako" Stone opens
his door to a mysterious woman without a past,
he knows his time off is over. As threats to Dee's
life bring her and Jacob together, she must set
aside her pride and accept the help of the military
hero with too many secrets of his own.

Out of Uniform
by Catherine Mann

Available February wherever you buy books.